MAIN STREET MASSACRE

Muzzle flashes erupted from under the porch roof of the Palace Saloon and hot lead sang. Cutter pumped a hard kick to the jasper's come-together, hinging him over, then grabbing his pard, crawfished and pulled the man behind the nearby horse-trough.

"Call off your dogs, mister or this man dies!" Cutter yelled.

The gunsels answered with more lead, missing Cutter but drilling their pard clear through the full trough. The man twitched grotesquely as the slugs cut into his belly and his dark blood flowed together with the leaking water.

Clenching his fist, Cutter powered up, grabbed the heavy body and ran toward the pair of shootists. As soon as he reached the walk, he heaved the dead man, knocking over one killer and forcing the other to run.

Cutter tossed off a shot and the outlaw threw up his arms, veering into the hitchrail. Backshot and bleeding, the man hit the rigid crossbar and somersaulted, coming down hard in the dust, stone dead at the hooves of the horse standing there.

ERNEST HAYCOX
IS THE KING OF THE WEST!

Over twenty-five million copies of Ernest Haycox's rip-roaring western adventures have been sold worldwide! For the very finest in straight-shooting western excitement, look for the Pinnacle brand!

RIDERS WEST   (17-123-1, $2.95)
by Ernest Haycox
Neel St. Cloud's army of professional gunslicks were fixing to turn Dan Bellew's peaceful town into an outlaw strip. With one blazing gun against a hundred, Bellew found himself fighting for his valley's life—and for his own!

MAN IN THE SADDLE   (17-124-X, $2.95)
by Ernest Haycox
The combine drove Owen Merritt from his land, branding him a coward and a killer while forcing him into hiding. But they had made one drastic, fatal mistake: they had forgotten to kill him!

SADDLE AND RIDE   (17-085-5, $2.95)
by Ernest Haycox
Clay Morgan had hated cattleman Ben Herendeen since boyhood. Now, with all of Morgan's friends either riding with Big Ben and his murderous vigilantes or running from them, Clay was fixing to put an end to the lifelong blood feud — one way or the other!

"MOVES STEADILY, RELENTLESSLY FORWARD WITH GRIM POWER."
— THE NEW YORK TIMES

CUTTER
PANHANDLE PAYBACK

DUFF McCOY

PINNACLE BOOKS
WINDSOR PUBLISHING CORP.

PINNACLE BOOKS

are published by

Windsor Publishing Corp.
475 Park Avenue South
New York, NY 10016

First printing: July, 1990

Printed in the United States of America

For Marilyn, my pard.

Chapter 1

The lash of the bullwhip snapped hard across the man's bare back, slamming him against the flogging post in the center of the prison yard. Another red welt added to the fiery crisscross pattern that oozed red droplets. The bound man twitched against ropes that pinned his arms wrenchingly aloft. A gasp of pain broke from him.

"Won't do it no more! Won't break yer rules!"

The words were animal-like barks in the sunbaked quadrangle between stone walls. Prisoners in baggy striped convicts' garb stood lined up to view the punishment, but the eyes of most of them fixed on the guards and their loaded shotguns.

"Hey, you yard birds! Watch the show! Unless you want *your* butts striped too?" The shouter's chest puffed like a pigeon's behind the vest that identified him as the warden's captain. "That weakling bastard at the post begged! That means extra kisses by the snake! Commence dishin' em', Mr. Boggs!"

The brawny turnkey wielding the fifteen-foot lash grinned wolfishly. Then his arm jerked, the plaited coil hissed, and the buckskin cracker popped, ripping into flesh. The flogged man's skin split in a shoulder-to-waist gash, and the leather came away bloody. It dragged on the gritty ground, leaped again as if alive. The next blow embedded the lash deeply, so it had to be jerked free.

The man screamed.

As the lash struck the prisoner again and again, flecks of skin flew and blood dyed the victim's torso red. He thrashed from tethered wrists like a hooked fish, and howled his agony.

In the ribbon of shade along the adobe administration building walked three men in civilian clothes. Two were neat, but the third one's trousers and shirt were ill-fitting and rumpled. The oldest — attired in a pressed suit of broadcloth — ignored the commotion and minced fussily toward the tall main gate. "Isaak Hines," he was saying, "your time here's about up. A few minutes from now you'll be outside these walls, a free man after nine long years. But I wonder if you've learned your lesson?"

Twenty yards away, the whip tore another shriek from the man at the punishment stake. Hines raised his voice to be heard. "Warden, you bet I have."

The prison guard walking beside the warden held a Winchester in the crook of his arm. He waved easy greeting to other rifle-carriers on the ramparts below which the threesome stopped. More guards on the ground flanked the gate. Their eyes were menacing in the desert glare.

The warden rocked on his heels, sweat dampening his short-trimmed mustache. He mopped his brow. "Hines, people like you are scum," the warden blurted. "A court found you guilty of brutal rape, but failed to sentence you to hang. Instead, you were locked up here. Now, I have a wife and daughter, Hines, and am a respecter of womanhood. Frankly, I'd rather see you

8

dead than walking this earth."

Hines's homely, pocked face twitched, but he said nothing and clenched both fists at his sides. He noticed the guards' half-raised Greeners with fingers glued on triggers. He knew that if he so much as scratched his ass he'd be shot in his tracks. Hines looked down sullenly. "Jes' let me go, warden, awright?"

On the distant hill, the sun winked on reflecting lenses. Hines glimpsed this, but at the moment his attention was engaged elsewhere. The warden sighed, gave a signal, and the gate opened a scant two feet. The hinges squeaked just as the flogged man renewed pained yells.

On the road outside the gate a battered wagon stood, and in the harness a fly-gnawed team of plugs. A prison handyman, not a guard, slouched on the warped seat. Hines shambled forward as if still wearing heavy leg irons, and climbed over the tailgate. The driver snapped his reins and the rig moved out, leaving the warden and other men scowling in the shade of the gray walls.

On the far hilltop a powerfully built man rolled from his prone position, brushing flinty dust from the shirt stretched by his broad shoulders. He stuffed battered field glasses into a leather case. The sunbrowned face was frozen and emotionless, and so, too, were the deeply set black eyes. The cruel cast to his mouth showed no reaction to the scene he'd witnessed. The lines of bitterness had been etched long ago.

The hair that showed below the stained hat with the rattler-skin band was lank and dark. The man's cheeks were unshaven from days on the trail. Now, with boots

9

sliding on the downslope, he turned from the prison he'd been watching since dawn. Beside a claw-branched clump of greasewood his bay gelding stood tied. Nearby a piebald mare snorted and stamped.

He tightened his cinch and loosened the Winchester in the worn, waxed saddleboot. Then he drew the Colt .44 Navy from the holster low on his hip. He checked the loads. The seven carved notches in the butt dug his palm familiarly. He holstered the weapon.

Time was passing, and he needed to be at the cross-road. He swung his frame into the saddle and gigged the bay. The spare horse trotted at lead.

The hot sun smote the boulder-strewn flat like an irresistible blazing fist. From distant east to distant west the level stage road arrowed, lost to view at hazed horizons; a purple sawtooth range glowered far to the north. One could have called this high desert a model of hell.

But Ike Hines didn't.

The gangling ex-convict stood in loose brogans and tight shirt at the intersection of the high road with the low road, the rutted track down which, hidden by terrain, the formidable prison squatted. Here was where its old supply wagon had dropped him to wait. Here was where he'd been told stagecoaches drove past often. Courtesy of the Territory of New Mexico, Hines's pocket held five crisp dollar bills. This was enough for his one-way fare, and a meal, or possibly two, when he reached a town.

But until rolling wheels brought transportation his way, he was a human afoot where humans afoot had no business: a land of scorpions, horned toads and sidewinders. The sun pounded down unmercifully. There was no shade.

A soaring buzzard swooped near, saw the erect man up and alive, then winged on. Hines had failed to conserve the water in the canteen he'd been left, and now suffered thirst. He'd never been one to plan ahead much.

Still, for all his discomfort, Hines was happy, for he was free. He peered at the dazzlingly blue afternoon sky and reckoned he'd been waiting in the sun for at least an hour. He scratched his itchy crotch, then his lopsided jaw. *If I had me a gun, I just could rob the stage, I calc'late,* he told himself. But Hines had no gun. The warden wasn't a particularly bright man, but he was no fool.

So the newly released prisoner passed the time stomping and mashing ants. The crumbly mound that was home to the red insects spilled out hundreds with each indentation by a toe. Ike Hines's shoe soles grew slimy and slick with his effort. Then he heard the clop-clop of approaching horses.

He looked around at the mount and its tall rider, seeing only featureless forms, starkly outlined against sun. Eerie rays beamed around the silhouette as it spoke: "Howdy, fella. Like being lonesome?"

Hines grunted. "Hell, no. Waitin' for a stage. Oughtta be one comin' by."

"Yeah?"

"Yeah."

"How often?"

Hines fought a mouth almost dry as sand. "For what?"

"How often are stages supposed to pass this way?"

Hines thought about it. "Dunno."

11

"One be along tomorrow, maybe? The day after?" The rider shifted, but not into better view. "You got enough water to drink, fella? Grub?"

"Naw."

The big horse fiddlefooted under the man who straddled him. Hines glimpsed a sixgun riding a hip. "Reckon you could use some help," the stranger offered in a gruff voice. "Got me a spare bronc at lead. Want to ride along?"

Ike Hines's face noticeably brightened. "Ain't got but a lone dollar to m' name, mister," he lied. "But I'll give her to you, you let me aboard that horse, and ride into town."

"A dollar'd do."

"We got us a deal, then!" Hines half ran to the standing piebald and started to mount.

"Hold on!"

There was latent menace in the voice, and the ex-convict spun around. "Hey! W-what you want, mister? You said—"

The rider walked his horse toward the man on foot. "No, fella, it was *you* done the saying. Claimed you had a dollar to spend." For the first time Hines saw the rider's face. His jaw dropped.

The features he gaped at might have been chiseled from solid granite. The handrolled cigarette that hung from his lips augmented the sinister look. The stranger was big—six-and-a-half feet in height, with massive shoulders tapering down to a lean waist. He seemed younger than his face looked.

"Sure, the dollar. I'll hand it to you this minute." From his pants he fished a bank note.

"Tuck it in my boot-top."

"Huh? Feared I'll try some trick?"

"Fella, I don't want no trouble. Hell, maybe I'll ride off, just leave you sweating."

"You headin' for them mountains, mister?"

A nod, definitely unfriendly.

"Here's the greenback. Like you said to, I'm puttin' it in your boot."

For the first time, the big man's grimness cracked in a half smile. "Mount up now, fella, and let's ride."

He'd put the bay to a trot before Hines lifted to the saddle, and the follower was forced to catch up. But soon Ike Hines was bouncing along at the big man's side.

He was swaying in a comfortable saddle. The hot, dry wind was more tolerable a bit above the ground. They'd be comfortable in timbered high country come nightfall, camped and with full bellies.

Hines hid a sly grin. As slick as Ike Hines was, it would be nothing tonight to filch the Bowie the stranger wore at his belt. Plant it between his ribs while he slept. Get that dollar back, plus gain ownership of the big man's firearms and broncs.

"Something funny, fella?" The words broke Hines's reverie.

"Naw." He rubbed his nose. "By the way, since we're goin' to be *amigos* from now on, my name's Hines. Ike Hines."

The man half grinned. "That so."

"So what's *your* handle, mister?"

No answer.

Over the wide desert badlands the pair rode, sweating until their clothes were stiff with salt.

By the time the sun was low in a brassy sky, they'd left the naked flats well behind and penetrated the foothills. The horses trod lush grama on a game trail

13

under junipers when the riders came to a stream.

"We goin' to make camp hereabouts?" Hines's tone was eager.

"Over by that deadfall." The pair let their mounts trot across the brookside swale.

"Why's this spot better'n another?" Ike Hines wondered.

Turning in the saddle and peeling lips back in a snarl, the big man launched a tremendous backhand blow. His knuckles met Hines's lips, hammering them into teeth, splitting them to drool bright blood. Hines was catapulted from the piebald's back and flung to the ground, where sharp branches raked his skin. Howling in pain, he tried to scramble off, but the stranger dismounted and grabbed him. Hines groaned.

"That all you got to say?" His fist busted Hines in the jaw. Arms windmilling, the ex-convict backpedaled into the huge downed cottonwood and crashed face first. He rolled to his feet to gape at his tormentor.

Nostrils smeared bloody crimson, Hines croaked: "What you got agin me? I never seen your mug afore today!"

The big man ranged close. "Yeah, you have."

"Sure as my name is Ike Hines, I—"

The big man had opened his shirt and yanked back the cloth. His chest was matted with dark, curled hair—except for an area just above the heart that bore a large, disfiguring scar.

"You ain't—?" Hines cringed. "Not after all them years! B-but the goddamn brand says it *is* you!"

Three inches above the nipple on his right side, the big man's broad chest had been hot-branded with the letter "C" inside a circle. The scar was rough and purplish, four inches across.

14

"Circle C! You're that Cutter boy, Jeb!" Ike Hines's scrawny form quaked. "Christ, what happened was over thirteen years ago!"

"Damned unlucky for you, I'd call it," Cutter rasped.

He drove his fist hard into the other man's gut, and watched him spin away, puking.

Chapter 2

"Oh, Jesus Christ, my head hurts!"

The scrawny ex-convict Ike Hines swam up from unconsciousness, overwhelmed at the way the tables had been turned. One minute he'd been planning a backstabbing that would harvest him weapons, put him back in business outlaw-style. The next, granite knuckles were battering his face and pounding his midsection blue. Now he tried to move his arms and legs, but failed, then saw why.

He was hogtied to the fallen tree trunk, rump and shoulderblades pressed to rotting wood. Termites scurried along his skin and under his clothes. The itching, together with the pain of tight ropes at wrists and ankles, was living hell.

His neck was wedged in a fork of branches, and his head couldn't turn. He was forced to look into the vicious eyes of Jeb Cutter, whom he'd known years back in Texas.

Thirteen years before.

The one whose pa he'd helped murder.

"Look, Cutter, I . . ."

The big Texan backhanded Hines. "Shut your face."

Cutter's scowl turned even more baleful. "I ain't seen you these thirteen years. Time we got acquainted."

16

He'd half turned away, busy with his hands. At exactly what, Hines couldn't see, and the fact caused him concern. Then Cutter stepped close and raised his well-used Colt by its barrel. Into the worn walnut butt grips were carved a number of notches. Hines was able to count seven.

"What you aimin' to do?"

"Talk some," Cutter said, poking his prisoner's neck with the gun.

Hines gulped hard, watching every move like a hawk.

A growl broke from the big man. "My pa died 'cause the rancher you ramrodded for, he wanted Circle C land that belonged to us!"

"Yeah, Bert Wendell wanted everybody's land. But—"

"Your outfit came raiding one day. Oh, I was young then, but I recollect. We were branding yearlings near our spring when Wendell's crew rode out of the trees. Figured to beat us up, but we fought back hard. Next thing I knew, Pa was on the ground with a bullet in him. I got knocked down, and some of you boys pinned me." Cutter wiped his hand across his brow. "Our branding iron was hot in the fire, so it must've looked like it'd be fun to mark me. And that's what you done!"

Ike's eyes were locked to the bared chest in front of him, and the ugly, disfiguring brand.

"The hot iron hurt like hell, Hines," he was saying, "and I could smell my flesh smoking while those cowhands held me so I couldn't move. But that was nothing to seeing my pa's shot-up body. My only kin."

"B-but, Wendell, he let you live—"

"You figure I don't know why? To show other small

17

ranchers what'd happen unless they sold out cheap." In Cutter's head the scenes from the past lived again in this moment. In his mind's eye he was again bolting from the grip of brutal cowhand gunsels, his chest hurting from battering and burns. Taking the chance he saw for himself, to reach the raiders' ground-hitched horses.

The nearest animal happened to be Wendell's favorite, a sleek stallion. Young Cutter had vaulted aboard and made a bold run for it across the open flatland. Only a bad fall brought horse and rider down.

Cutter had been dragged to town and turned over to a hostile sheriff. The trial they'd held had been quick and direct: the Wendell-influenced jury found him guilty of horse stealing; the Wendell-bought judge sentenced him to ten years in the state pen. And the stuffed frock coat had called himself lenient, since horse thieves by rights deserved hanging.

The judge claimed hard labor would cure lawlessness in the kid.

"Heard tell you got a pardon."

Cutter shrugged. "I saved the warden's life when some of the lifers took him hostage to stage a break. By that time I'd seen in newspapers how the bastard Bert Wendell got killed. In a Kiowa raid on Bitter Wash, the town he'd founded. By the time I got out from behind bars in Texas, you were in the New Mexico pen. Nine years for rape."

"A sweet young piece—"

"Shut up!" Cutter snarled. "Hines, I been watching calendars. I made sure I was on the prison road when you'd be freed. I suckered you. But being a fool don't buy you mercy, fella. Now comes payback time."

Beads of sweat on the bound man's brow broke and

rivered into his eyes. The vomit-streaked face contorted, and the tears welled. Hines tried to squirm, uselessly. "You aim to shoot pieces off'n me?"

Cutter stepped back, thumbed the pistol's hammer and drew his bead. "If you hadn't kept me waiting so long, I wouldn't be ornery."

"Cutter! Wait!"

"Compare this with chest-branding!" He pointed the Colt's barrel at Hines's heart.

"Don't shoot! Bert Wendell wasn't killed by Injuns! He's alive!" Ike Hines bellowed, and the words made Cutter pause.

"What?"

"You was knocked out in that fight with the ranch raiders, remember? You woke up and seen your pa was dead. Well, Bert Wendell, he was the one pulled the trigger! And Wendell, not me, pressed hot iron onto your hide!"

"You claiming Wendell ain't dead?"

"The 'Bert Wendell' that got Injun-killed, he was the uncle of the man that done in your pa. Just an old cuss, but his death got told in newspapers all over Texas. But the man who killed your pa—" It occurred to Ike Hines to hold his tongue.

"You don't need to spell it out." Cutter sighed. "You're willing to tell where Wendell is and what he's up to. But you won't if you're dead."

The head wedged between tree branches attempted to nod. "I heard plenty things, Cutter, even locked up in the pen. Cut these here ropes off me, we'll cook some grub, palaver whilst we fill our bellies. We'll be pards from now on."

"Fella, I could beat what I want out of you."

"With me healthy, I could put you face-to-face with

19

Wendell. He's a gent as don't cotton to strangers gettin' past the guards he keeps."

"All right, we'll deal."

Ten minutes later the pair hunkered beside a campfire that flickered in the failing day. A dented coffeepot sat on a wire spider over the flames and steamed. Cutter was rummaging in a saddlebag, laying out airtights of beans and chunks of oilskin-wrapped salt pork. Tall lodgepole pines cast shadows that deepened the dusk.

The loudest sound was the murmuring of Ike Hines's rasping voice. He talked in rambling fashion, holding things back.

Cutter's life had been hard and bitter since Bert Wendell had destroyed family, freedom, land. The Texas prison he'd been thrown into was tough, and the kid had served two years. His back was scarred by whippings, and his chest wore the brand. But breaking rocks with a sledge *had* put muscle on him, and he'd grown up fast and mean.

After his release, he'd taken to roaming ways, knowing the Circle C was gone, built over by the new town of Bitter Wash. He never bothered to return to old ground. He'd learned to use weapons with deadly efficiency from a Mexican he'd shared a shack with in the Indian Nation. And since old Ruiz was versed in Comanchero ways, distrust for all law rubbed off as well.

And indifference to folks who left him alone, hate for those who crossed him — or tried to.

"So I get you close to Wendell," Ike Hines now said. "Then you can carve him for dirty things he done. Hell, you came up tough. You taken the owlhoot trail?"

Cutter shot him a look, wishing it were a bullet.

"Figure that's your business?"

"Hell, no."

Hines fumbled with sticks he was feeding the fire. "I won't talk of nothin' you don't care to, pard." Cutter noted the man's restless pig eyes. They kept roaming to his holstered Colt. And the Bowie at his belt. And the Winchester beside his grounded saddle.

"The coffee smells good and strong, pard," Hines said casually. "Reckon I'll have me a tin cupful. Mind?"

Cutter nodded his head and continued groping in the saddlebag. Hines picked up the pot, then popped the lid and hurled the hot brew at Cutter's face.

Cutter sidelonged, avoiding most of the scalding liquid. But Hines had snatched up a rock the size of his fist, leaped the fire with surprising spryness, and slammed the sandstone chunk at the big man's head.

The blow was glancing. Cutter brought his hand up, saddlebag and all, and struck his attacker as he passed. Hines's legs folded as if made of wet paper, and he catapulted into the fire. His shirt went up in flames and, screeching hideously, he flopped on his back as his skin blistered and turned crisp. He looked down to see the gaping stab wound in his ribcage gushing thick blood.

Cutter shook off the leather bag he'd shoved his deadly hideout weapon through to skewer the man. Now, he raised his Marston knife-blade gun: a pocket pistol with sharp blade affixed, alongside three stacked derringer's barrels. Cutter wiped the blade in long grass without hurry, then slipped it back in its boot sheath.

The stink of the scorching corpse threatened to spoil the campsite, and with night fully fallen, moving

21

would be a chore. Cutter took hold of Hines's ankles and yanked him from the fire. He debated with himself how far to drag the corpse, decided that the main thing was not needing to look at it, and let it lie in a heap. He ambled to the horses and adjusted their picket pins.

"Damn fool!" Cutter grunted.

Returning to the fire, he tossed dry branches on it, set the bean can near the heat, and dropped meat in his tin pan. Soon the smell of cooking food neutralized the death stink. Hot grub went down fast and easy.

His mind raced over what he'd discovered in the last hour. His father's killer—the same man who'd branded his chest—was alive. Cutter's brain swarmed with vengeful thoughts. As he chewed stale biscuit, he fingered the brand ridges on his chest. He knew already he'd have no rest until he'd done for Bert Wendell.

The most likely thing, it occurred to Cutter, was that Bert Wendell had stayed put on his old stomping grounds—Bitter Wash, Texas, and the rangeland around that cowtown. But that was a long way from where the big man hunkered tonight. Cutter knew how much money he had in his poke: seven dollars, plus small change—and that was counting the dollar note Hines had contributed. But just maybe Hines could provide him with more. . . .

The lean face emotionless, he tugged the makings from his shirt pocket—papers and muslin-sacked Dixie Queen tobacco. While studying his next move, he carefully built a quirly. He lit it with an ember-ended stick from the fire, then moved to his saddle near the corpse. In the flickering firelight he took his second saddlebag, the one stocked with clothes and cartridges. He drew out a packet of folded papers and began leafing through them, squinting first at printed words and pictures, then at Hines's remains.

Minutes passed. Then, holding one of the paper sheet, he stepped near the corpse and squinted carefully at it. He finally nodded and stuffed the flier in the pocket of his shirt. He drew the knife from his belt sheath and tested the blade on his thumb. It was razor sharp. Cutter dropped to his knees and grabbed the dead cheeks between his fingers. The scorched skin was slick and insisted on shredding, but he held the dead head tight as he put the Bowie into play.

He placed the keen edge at the base of the nose. He sliced skin and flesh till he met resistance, then forced the blade back and forth, sawing through cartilage. There was a sound like a breaking matchbox, and then bone parted; the nose came away to roll on the turf like a toy.

Cutter cocked his head as the smoke from the quirly curled about his face, and studied his handiwork, frowning. Laying the knife on a flat stone, he moved into position to heft the body. The fire now smoldered, which satisfied him. After checking the pockets and finding the other four greenbacks, he grabbed Hines beneath the arms, felt the slippage of loose, dead flesh, but managed to pitch the corpse headfirst on the bed of coals.

A puff of smoke and sweetish stench went up, and the remains of the fire darkened and smothered. Cutter left the head in the fire while he counted to twenty, then used a foot to kick the corpse away to lie grotesquely face-up. There was still enough light to see. The face without a nose was tattered and mashed from brow to chin, the lips drawn back like rawhide strips, eyeballs melted in sockets.

23

"That'll do." He flipped away the spent quirly.

He moved upwind of the dead man to spread his soogans and bed down. Back in the forest, owls hooted softly. A distant wolf howled. Overhead spread a pattern of brilliant stars.

Cutter dropped off lightly, as usual, his hand near the notched butt of his sixgun. But no threat woke him, and he slept soundly in the mountain night.

Chapter 3

The big Texan saw the town from far on the flats: a clutch of unpainted, raw buildings squatting under a high, hot sky. He gigged the bay past a dancing dust devil, the mare at lead shying. But then, the piebald had been edgy all day.

Amid the bird twittering of the mountain daybreak Cutter had loaded Ike Hines's corpse. He'd used strong force bending it to the mare's saddle, breaking the rigor-set bones where needed, using a reata and achieving a good, taut snub. But it wasn't a shifting load that distressed the beast; it was the fact that the load stank. The putrid scent of death radiated far in the heat of the desert. Alerted buzzards gliding upper air currents coasted low. Scavenger coyotes skulked in greasewood clumps, pointed muzzles twitching.

The rider leading the pack animal kept a straight, slow path toward town. The trackless ground turned to a rutted roadway, and then to a street between buildings bearing weathered signs. Cutter's gaze raked the Babylon Saloon, the Golden Spike Saloon, the Yellow Garter Saloon. There was a hole-in-the-wall café and a tumbledown blacksmith's barn.

The shabbiest place in view wore a shingle that announced:

Cutter drew rein, the bay halted, and the piebald drew alongside. The few passersby on the boardwalk raised curious eyes. A mangy dog crept close, sniffing.

Swinging down from his saddle, he mounted the jailhouse steps and shouldered open the door. The badge-packer had planted his bulk in a chair tipped back to the wall. His watery eyes came open and the chin locked to block a yawn. "Mister, this close to the border I come to honor the *siesta* habit the Mexicans got. It's midday, so if ya care to flap your jaws later—"

Cutter tipped back his hat and shook his head.

The lawman shook his head, disbelieving. "Listen, mister, it's Marshal Wade Loggins as is tellin' you—"

"I'm here now, lawman," Cutter said coldly. His glittering eyes hardened the rugged face still more. "And it's business, or I wouldn't bother. Reward business."

"You're a bounty hunter?"

"Been known to dabble."

"Jesus!"

The front legs of the chair came down and Wade Loggins stiffened to his feet. He was flabby and his vest fit him like a sausage skin. Pulling his trousers up over his gut, he walked around the scarred oak desk. "Well," he said, yawning, "fetch what you got in and I'll ask him about hisself. I take it he ain't confessin' to his sins?"

"Saying nothing, that's true."

"I'll wait here."

"If it's what you choose." Cutter stalked outside, where a curious crowd had bunched, pointing and talking.

Cutter was big enough to carry the corpse easily, the muscles rippling under his shirt as he crossed the

26

threshold with townsfolk trailing. He dropped Hines's stiff, doubled-over form with a thud on the doorstep, and its rotten stench spread through the room. The spectators made sour faces and grumbled, but didn't leave. "This here's the bargain on paper, Marshal." He thrust a dog-eared wanted dodger at Loggins.

"Christ!" The lawman winced. "You brung that dead body in here? One so far gone?" The office was shoulder-to-shoulder with excited people, and growing stuffier. Sweat poured down Loggins's face. "You got to take it back outside, mister."

"Read the paper." Cutter's voice was edged with steel.

"Oh, awright."

The lawman perused the flier and looked up, puzzled. "No-Nose Kibbee, the bank robber? Two hundred dollar reward?"

" 'Dead or Alive.' "

The marshal scratched his chin. "Can't give you no money!"

"Money's what I came for," Cutter said evenly. "This here's the town of Pecos. Some months back the Pecos Bank got robbed."

"This body, it's messed up too bad." Wade Loggins cleared his raspy throat. "Can't be identified proper. Looks like it fell in a fire. That's your first problem, Bounty Man. 'Tother one is, the reward's the banker's, not mine. And I don't guess Mr. Elihu Horvelle'll be available, under the circumstances."

Cutter stared at Marshal Loggins. The look was long, cold, and bordering on the sinister. The deep-set eyes met those of the meaty lawman, and the lawman's slid away. Loggins peered into the crowd — all merchants and ribbon-clerk types — and saw no help for himself.

27

He licked his slack lips.

"Oh, awright, I'll send for Horvelle." But before he could make a move, through the crush pushed a stick-thin older man in a black clawhammer coat. The gent wagged his flowing goatee as he stepped up. "No need to send for me, Wade. I'm here. Not too entirely occupied with ledgers to care what's happening in the town. I heard of some excitement, and—" The full impact of the decaying dead man struck the banker. "Oh, my God!"

"Fella claims this here's No-Nose Kibbee," Loggins explained. "Wants to collect the bounty. Well, this corpse ain't got a nose, that's true, but it's a small man's body, and Kibbee was tall. I," the marshal stated, "say no reward gets paid."

"If there's doubt," the banker agreed, "no. No reward." Then he felt his neck prickle as Cutter's stare fell on him. "Mister," Horvelle said, "it was my bank as got held up. This dead critter don't resemble the bandit."

"He's got no nose."

"Sorry." Horvelle turned to go.

Cutter blocked his path. "Mister, the wanted flier says two hundred'll be paid. I went to the trouble to fetch this hunk of meat in." The dark eyes of the big man narrowed.

"Two hundred dollars is a lot," Elihu Horvelle said, running fingers through his chinwhiskers. Worried at the change of atmosphere, folks were starting to scatter.

Marshal Loggins had taken a step toward the glass-paneled gun cupboard. Cutter's hand draped near the notched gun butt as latent violence hung in the air.

Loggins's hand brushed the sixgun he wore, but leapt away of its own accord. When the lawman spoke, his voice was reedy. "You'd best clear out, Bounty Man. There's no payoff for you here." The marshal's shirt was sweated wet, and his hands shook.

"I don't meet up with too many folks willing to cheat a man like me," Cutter said. A casual move of his hand brought his Bowie out; then he used it to pare a fingernail. "But when I do . . ." His stare didn't falter as it swept Loggins and the quaking Horvelle. Suddenly Cutter turned and drove the blade hard down into the desk top, pinning the dodger on No-Nose Kibbee there. "It ain't pretty!"

"Er—" the marshal began. "Now, you just see here, mister—"

"Wade," Horvelle interrupted, "I . . . uh . . . am grateful for this stranger's bringing Kibbee here to the only justice he deserves. He's got a right to the money." The banker reached into his coat and withdrew a billfold. His old features seemed to have aged ten years. "Here!" He tossed a wad of greenbacks beside the knife that quivered in the desk.

"Obliged," Cutter said, pocketing the bills, then restoring the knife to its sheath. But his face stayed fierce as he stepped to the flyspecked window and jerked it up. "I'll be on my way now. And feeling some better about the good nature of you folks." Dropping to the ground, he skirted the crowd at the front door and strode toward the horses.

"Hold on!"

A raw-looking young man with peach-fuzz cheeks and tattered duds slipped from the alley, and determined strides put him in Cutter's path. He confronted the big man with a sneer on his baby face. "I wasn't inside the jail just now," he snarled, clutching a tattered slouch hat to the front of his britches. "But from what folks say, you just collected the Kibbee reward. No-

29

Nose weren't such a bad *hombre*, y' know. Just a mite sour about the saloon fight that ruint his looks. I was his kid brother, stranger—"

He let the hat fall and pointed the gun it concealed, an old .36 Confederate Schneider and Glassick. The piece was rusty, but primed, and the hammer was drawn back. The kid's eyes spat angry fire.

"Now, who went and lied to you like that, son?"

"W-why, Joe, the swamper at the Spi—" His close-set eyes wavered and glanced away. It was the last move he made in life. Cutter drew his Colt with rattle-snake-like speed, fanning it as it came level to buck and boom. The speeding slug drilled the kid's breast-bone, lung and heart, hurling him backward as the faded shirt blossomed crimson. Then, he pitched in the street among the horse.

A rush of stinking body waste fouled the breeze.

Cutter held his smoking .44 as the crowd re-formed about him. It took only two seconds for the marshal to break through.

"You—"

"Calm down, Loggins," Cutter said slowly, putting up his weapon and walking toward where his gelding waited patiently. "Self-defense. Those that saw it are bound to agree."

"I sure wish you'd clear outa town, stranger."

"I aim to." He heaved into the saddle of his gelding, tugged the reins of the piebald and moved off.

"Ain't it the bounty hunter as collected the reward?" a townsman wondered.

"Greased lightning with a gun. No wonder he brung No-Nose down."

"That wouldn't ha' been so tough. The kid was the brother with the fast draw!"

Soon the comments were drowned by distance and

30

the clop of hooves. As Cutter rode, he lit a quirly with a sulfur match, and inhaled deep. Behind lay the town of Pecos, and ahead, the Pecos River. Beyond that, most of the Lone Star State stretched, the Texas-land where he'd been raised.

It must have changed in thirteen years. And he'd change it more before he'd spent the stake he'd raised.

Chapter 4

He spent some of the reward on grub at a trader's store on the edge of the badlands, then bought ammunition in the farther-along cowtown of Steerville. He kept the gelding's nose pointed due east after riding past abandoned old Fort Douglass, and forded the Brazos in a storm rampant with wild winds and sheeting rain.

Although he crossed country known for Indian troubles, he saw no red men, warlike or otherwise, and rode determinedly through the stoked-hot summer days. A man accustomed to constant vigilance, he scanned the horizons—and all land between—with eyes that were restless and wary.

The lessons of Cutter's past had been hard learned: you spotted trouble while it was still far off, else you'd need to face it close up, inevitably. If it hadn't already killed you unawares. So it wasn't fear, but habit, that put the edginess in the big man's eyes. It was the same habit that for years, on dangerous trails he wandered, had allowed him to survive.

And Jeb Cutter had never wanted to survive more than now, with his longed-for vengeance so near. He at last knew the identity of the hated slayer of his father, and felt in his bones that he was getting close to him.

He could almost feel his hands wrapping around the bastard's throat, hear his cowardly squeals. He'd pay slow and dear.

Gradually the terrain changed from desert plain to grassland, and longhorns became plentiful, grazing in small bunches or in larger herds. The traveler encountered smoke plumes from ranch chimneys more frequently, but he never veered from his straight-on route. When the country grew familiar and boyhood memories started to crowd, he set his face rigid and only pushed his mount more.

At a tree-shaded winding stream that cut the broad grassland, he dismounted and let the horses water, then eased his frame down to sit on the bank. The Winchester—a fairly new weapon—he wiped free of dust and oiled, but not to excess. Then he worked with his handguns, starting with the Colt. He spread a bandanna on a flat rock, removed the shells from the trusty gun, examining each and laying them aside. He used rod and rag on the bore until it shone, dry-fired on an empty cartridge, not harming the delicate firing pin. The action was crisp and clean. Finally he filmed the gun lightly with oil and reloaded.

Then it was the hideout gun's turn.

At this point his face turned thoughtful.

He held the gleaming W. Marston derringer in his hand and hefted its bulk. He used his fingers to extend and then retract the sliding knife blade riding beside the barrels. The over-under three-shot .22 had a history he didn't entirely know. The weapon had belonged to old Ruiz when he'd met the Indian-Mexican half-breed.

Cutter hadn't thought of Ruiz for weeks, although every moment of every day he lived by the habits the wily old fox had implanted in him. Ruiz, as a young man, had ridden with Comancheros, actually been

33

one of those most feared outlaws of the southwest plains. He had done his share of robbing, killing, even selling guns and firewater to redskins. Plus abducting settlers' kids and women to auction below the Rio Grande as slaves.

In his prime, Ruiz had led a lusty, notorious life. But as an old man, he'd been alone, starved, sick and hurting.

Cutter, fresh out of Texas prison and broke, had come on Ruiz in a ramshackle wilderness shack. The old man had broken a leg in a fall, was two-thirds starved and fading fast. Cutter shot game to feed the old timer, and managed to bring him back to health. Ruiz never did say so much as "thank you" to the boy. But there was the Comanchero code of paying off a debt that the old man honored. And he paid Cutter, then not yet out of his teens, with the only valuable thing he could: skills.

In the more than two years the pair spent together in the rugged redrocks of the Indian Territory, Cutter learned the wilderness skills of hunting and tracking. Being half Mescalero, Ruiz knew the red man's ways. Cutter soon learned how to stalk like an Indian, use the bow and arrow, get along on little water and even less food.

Kill with his hands as well as shoot rifles and pistols with great marksmanship and speed. Use the silent, deadly garrote to strangle foes.

Now Cutter, recalling those years, turned the Marston pistol over in his hands, then shoved it in the hideout scabbard sewn in his boot. He saw the horses were eagerly cropping grass, so he grabbed the makings and rolled a short, fat quirly. Then he peered up past leafy treetops at the fleece-clouded sky.

It had been such a day as this when Ruiz had finally died, a death as violent as the early life before Jeb

Cutter had become his *compadre*. As it happened, Cutter had been forced to witness the killing, unable to prevent it. The patrol of cavalry bluecoats had ridden up to the shack when he was off hunting, attempted to arrest the old man and met resistance.

They'd gotten off on the wrong foot by shooting his pet coyote, Pepe. The captain of the patrol had ordered Ruiz dragged away. They tried to hold the old man down to club him with their rifle butts, but he rushed the officer, who'd finished him with his saber.

From a rimrock far beyond rifle range Cutter had watched the incident through a spyglass. When Ruiz was skewered he'd considered rampaging down and confronting the bluebellies outright—but he'd abandoned the hopeless cause. Ruiz had told him many times never to battle impossible odds, but survive to fight other days. So Cutter had survived that moment, but picked off three pony soldiers with his rifle before they could leave the canyon. Only then had he returned to bury Ruiz.

And take for his own the fine Colt sixgun that had been Ruiz's pride. The one carrying the seven notches in its butt.

Cutter had ridden in bitterness ever since, hating the law, hating the army, but at least he'd ridden armed and able to take care of himself.

Now, today, the bay and piebald were rested, and he got up from hunkering in the grass and went to climb into the saddle.

Bitter Wash was waiting.

He wondered if Bert Wendell still looked the same. Maybe prosperity and comfort had turned him flabby. Cutter smiled and touched his Colt.

There existed no layers of fat or broadcloth that could stop .44 slugs.

* * *

The next day's lowering lead-gray sky attempted a drizzle before it cleared off at midmorning, the blue vault of sky returning bright as usual, and the sun hurling down its heat and glare. The temperature rose as rapidly as Cutter's eagerness as he rode the last few miles toward Bitter Wash. He knew the town's location because it occupied the very land his pa, Enoch, had built his ranch on all those years ago. Where the old Circle C headquarters structures had sat now supposedly reared saloons, stores and all the businesses of the typical cowtown.

He'd not returned to the place since being driven off to prison in a barred cage balanced on a wagon box. There'd been a gang of sullen waddies and an exultant Wendell to see him off. The local sheriff had been a sodden drunk—maybe still was, unless he'd turned up his pickled toes and died. Cutter despised them all, and if any crossed his path, he aimed to do for them.

Cutter knew that beyond the next line of hump-backed hills lay the town, and that he'd reach there before nightfall. But the horses needed water, and he could do with a bite of grub—and some rest out of the saddle. He remembered a sweet spring in a nearby gulch under some pleasant cottonwoods. The water accumulated in a pool, and had been the coldest and the best tasting in all Texas.

He turned the bay onto a familiar trail, and the gelding needed little urging. The fresh scent of damp grass hung on the breeze. The piebald mare followed at a trot, her spotted head held high.

Cutter cut the stream fifty yards below the pool, and stopped short. Peering through the trees, he saw a pair of saddle broncs tethered in thick graze. They cropped grass in a glade downwind, unaware of the big man's presence or his mounts'. He dismounted and tied his own horses at a loaf-shaped shelf of chalkstone beyond the chestnut and the roan. He began his advance over the carpet of leaves that covered the soft turf.

The big man scrambled in a low, doubled-over run, his best Indian moves sneaking him forward unseen and unheard. He reached the high ground overlooking the spring and pool, and flopped belly-down atop a boulder the size of a house. Then, squinting against the shimmer of sun-sheened water, he scanned the area about and below. The pool was fifteen or so feet across, and sage and berry bushes surrounded the blue expanse. Cutter gazed at the soft earth of the water's edge, then spotted the footprints.

Two people had walked to the boulder's base, just under his position. Cutter heard a thump, and a gasp of breath, then quiet. Unnatural quiet. Birds and animals were keeping still. Everything seemed frozen in place.

He rolled to his feet and moved down a nearby deer path, emerging a dozen feet below and to his left. Then he heard a woman's cry. He dropped to his haunches and cupped his gun handle with his hand.

Under the shrubbery a couple lay on a coarse blanket, the woman on bottom, the man on top. The woman was nearly naked, her head haloed in a cloud of yellow hair, her full breasts exposed. Between her slim legs locked at the ankles around his hips, a man pumped roughly, pounding her against the earth. He was average in height, but heavily muscled, and his solid weight battered her.

Cutter relaxed his grip and took a long drink from the pool.

In the shrubs the pumping man grunted in climax, collapsing across the woman, and lay still. After a minute both stirred. Cutter slid farther behind the bushes.

"There, Max Donovan," the woman's sobbing voice

said, "you've got what you wanted."

"Yeah, and I admit what ya claimed was true. You was cherry—up till t'day, that is! Haw!" There was the rustle of leaves as he dragged the woman upright and ran rough hands over her breasts, pinching her nipples cruelly, then turned to hike up his pants.

"So, how'd you end up likin' it, gal? Not much? Too bad. Me, I gotta be gettin' back t' town."

"And me to my father's ranch." An awkward pause followed. "Good day to you, then, Mr. Donovan."

Instead of answering, he sauntered to where the roan was tied, tightened the cinch and mounted.

A bit chain jingled and a hoof loudly stamped. "You'll keep your part of the bargain, won't you, Mr. Donovan? I mean—?"

"I know what ya mean, gal," Donovan said.

"My family and our place—?"

"Thanks for the good time, Em'ly, honey! If'n ya want more, ever, leave your message in the stump. *Adios!*" The mount was forced into sudden movement, likely by vicious spurring.

The pounding of hoofbeats receded, and there was quiet in the gulch. Then the sound of loud retching began. Cutter turned his head and saw the woman vomiting greenish slime in the grass. When the woman called Emily had finished, she straightened and made for the pool, shedding her last few garments. She entered knee-deep water a few yards from Cutter and began scrubbing herself. She scooped handfuls of gritty bottom sand, rubbed the grains on her cream-white skin, across her breasts and between blood-stained thighs.

Cutter stood up, stretched cramped muscles. When he started toward his horses, the woman caught sight of him and screamed.

Splashing to the bank, she ran for her pile of clothes

and came up with a sixgun.

He saw how plain of face she was, and how voluptuous of body, but there was chance for little more. The mother-naked woman triggered the Remington, aimed directly at Cutter's heart.

Chapter 5

Cutter threw himself swiftly to his right, sidelonging low, and dove below the speeding slug's path as it tugged the bandanna at his neck. He collided with the naked woman, and they both fell rolling in the grass beside the pond bank. Emily squirmed and fought furiously, trying to bring the pistol back into play. The steel barrel rapped the big man's brow, and drew blood.

He grabbed the Remington, locking its cylinder with his callused palm. The woman squealed in his ear, released the gun, and clawed at his eyes. Flinging her on her back, he pinned her arms, but her lower body bucked and plunged. Her knee made impact with his groin. He grunted and dropped on her, dirt-caked clothes grinding her tender skin.

"You ain't going to win this fight, lady," Cutter rasped. "May's well stop battling."

"You beast! You be—"

He struck her face once, and then again with the flat of his hand. Her head was jerked back like a rag doll's. Her gleaming teeth cut her lip and blood dribbled down. Her body went limp.

"All right, have your way with me if you wish," she sobbed. "You can't be any more despicable than

Donovan. Damn you! Damn all men!"

Cutter released his grip on the woman as he rocked back on his heels and rose. The move left the unclothed form stretched on the grassy bank, drops of water from her dip in the pond gleaming on her skin. He saw she wasn't as young as first he'd thought, somewhere in her late twenties. She seemed surprised at his retreat from her, and tried to cover herself with her hands. "Aren't you going to rape me?"

"Not likely," Cutter said and took to brushing the mud off his pants.

Puzzled, Emily watched the big man walk toward the bank where his two horses were tied.

"I suppose I should apologize for trying to shoot you," she said humbly. "You seem to have meant no harm. But you came on me of a sudden, you'll admit—"

"It ain't so, lady. Was on that bank quite a while."

"Oh! You were there when Mr. Donovan and I were—? And you didn't make yourself known?"

"Wasn't my affair, ma'am."

The plain features frowned. "Now *you're* misjudging *me!* I'm not what you think!"

"Not much guesswork about what I seen."

"Oh!"

The shapely legs twitched, and Emily gave a small jump. "I forgot I'm not dressed! Goodness!" She was suddenly blushing from toes to hairline. Her green eyes were distressed and shocked. "Yes, go ahead and be on your way! Now I've got to slip into my clothes. Sir, if you'll only turn your back—"

He shook his head. "I aim to head where them two horses are tied, but I don't turn my back on a loaded

41

gun."

"Oh! Insufferable!"

By the time he'd ambled to the trees and rock shoulder she'd struggled into her fringed riding skirt and a man's small shirt. She jammed a perky widebrim atop her curls as she set off in the same direction as Donovan. Cutter interrupted his horses' grazing to cinch their saddles tight and mount.

His own stomach was urging him to get to town, find a café and treat himself to a hot meal.

He was about to spur off when Emily's call rang out. "Oh, mister! Mister!"

He held taut rein as the woman ran up frantically.

"My horse is gone! That bastard Donovan must have drove it off! You've got to let me ride with you!"

Cutter didn't answer.

She stamped a tiny foot. "I've no way to get back home but hike shank's mare, and I'm in a hurry. I have a problem, I think." The green eyes had grown large and pleading.

"I'm heading for Bitter Wash. If the direction's right, jump up on the piebald."

"I'll ask my brother to pay for your help."

"Suit yourself."

She swung into the saddle and faced Cutter. Her teeth fastened on her lower lip worriedly. "Can we hurry? I'll explain on the way."

"I didn't suppose that I'd get lucky and you wouldn't see fit."

The pair set off at a trot, and the woman rattled on urgently. "I want to tell you about Donovan, so you won't carry the wrong idea about me. By the way, my name is Emily Vandermeer. And you're—?"

42

"Cutter."

She looked doubtfully at the man with the hostile manner. "Mr. Cutter, then. I live on a small ranch just this side of Bitter Wash. My two brothers have run the Spade 8 since my father died last year. Dave is twenty, Joe is eighteen, and they're hard-working young men whose desire is to hold on to the place and build up its herd. I couldn't bear it if anything happened to them."

Cutter rode silently, paying attention. Anything at all that pertained to Bitter Wash could turn out useful in his vengeance quest.

"That's why . . ." she hesitated. "That's why I did what I did with Max Donovan. I never did anything like it before, but if I didn't, he'd . . ."

"Afraid you're losing me, Emily Vandermeer."

"Don't you see, it was a payoff that I made! The bigshot who owns the town and most of the land roundabout wants our ranch too! There was to be a raid on the Spade 8 tonight, and I don't want my brothers killed! Donovan's the ramrod, said he'd stop short of killing them if I'd lie with him."

Cutter nodded. "Who's this kingpin fella?"

"Wendell. Bert Wendell, a ruthless man who employs a small army of gunfighters. He lives in a mansion on the tallest hill in Bitter Wash and runs his empire from there. Never comes outside without his crew of guards."

The man's obsidian eyes grew hard. "You say your spread ain't far?"

"Just down this trail."

"Might be best if we galloped a spell."

* * *

43

The horses were lathered and winded when Jeb Cutter and Emily Vandermeer rode over the last low ridge to spot a telltale smoke spire in the sky. Both had the feeling that they were already too late. The grove of birch on the slope into the ranch yard hid the sad story till they broke from the woods and onto a grassy strip. As soon as they were in the open, Cutter hauled reins and dragged the bay to a haunches-down halt.

To counterpoint his silence the woman burst out with a shocked gasp. "My God! The raiders have been here! Those bodies on the ground—my brothers."

The motionless forms lay between the house and the well. Beyond them, the gate of the pole corral was open and the remuda gone. The barn had been torched and crumbled in flames. No wrongdoers were in sight.

Cutter slid the Winchester from its saddleboot.

"My brothers may be still alive! At least one of them might!" Emily brushed tears from her plain, grief-ravaged face, and bent her body to spur the horse down the slope.

"Lady, I wouldn't—" Cutter began, but there was no point in finishing. A shot rang from the hilltop opposite, fired from long range, the weapon an awesomely powerful Sharps "Big Fifty." The buffalo gun hurled a slug that shattered the woman's arm as she rode, drilled her side and churned lungs and heart to soup. As her mount went down, she pitched from the saddle in a grotesque cartwheel, blood pumping from both entrance and exit holes. The corpse hit the ground and plowed sod with a broken face. Emily Vandermeer lay a misshapen heap in a crimson pool. Black flies began to buzz around her body.

Cutter didn't wait for a second shot, but spurred the bay and galloped toward the ranch stead. The mount leaped one man's sprawled corpse cleanly, and the big man noted that the victim had been shot in the back. The bay's forehooves smashed the other Vandermeer brother's head and sent a shower of brain matter scattering.

Cutter rode on.

As horse and rider passed the well in the ranch yard at a full-out run, another slug zipped and punched the suspended bucket, flinging it like a teacup in a gale. Cutter urged his mount around a toolshed and up the slope. He knew neither bushwhacker nor his motives, only that the rifle he used was single-shot. That meant he had precious seconds in which to reach the bastard, circle him and come at him from above.

The outcrop above the Sharps shooter was shattered granite, the footing poor. As the reined-in bay skidded to a stop, Cutter was out of the saddle and into a sprint. His boots slipped on detritus, but he kept his legs pumping till he stood tall on the rim.

He saw the bushwhacker directly below, a wiry man in puncher's garb, prying on the breech of a weapon that appeared jammed. Bending his shoulder to a precariously balanced boulder, Cutter heaved just as the rifleman glanced up, eyes wide with fear. The great stone lump tottered momentarily, then overturned with a crash and hurtled downward. The man lay prone, screaming in pain.

Cutter scrambled down the path chewed by the miniature avalanche and knelt beside the jasper. The lower body and both legs of the injured man were crushed under the mass of rock.

"Listen here," Cutter yelled over the man's anguished groans. "Did Bert Wendell pay your pards to burn this here spread?"

"Christ, the pain!" the half-crushed man raved. "Yeah, it was that bastard Wendell. I can't hardly stand it! Shoot me, mister! I'm beggin' you! Take away the pain!"

The big man regarded him. The jasper was bleeding from his ears and the corners of both eyes. His bearded cheek was caved in where it pushed against the ledge's stone floor. He began shrieking mindlessly. Cutter just snorted and turned away.

He hiked back to his horse and lifted to the saddle, the animal skittish at the hideous cries that filled its ears. The cries grew fainter as Cutter backtracked across the flat to where the fallen piebald lay. As he approached, he saw that the mare's stumble had broken a foreleg. He drew his Colt and fired once to put her out of misery. The horse shuddered once, then died.

Cutter continued toward the yard between the ranch buildings, above which several buzzards were already drifting low. The big man was weary, and the matter of three shot-up bodies confronted him unpleasantly.

He'd not been acquainted with the youths who now lay outstretched in death in the yard, and he'd known their sister only slightly. Still, she'd given him a clue to the situation he could expect to find in Bitter Wash, about Bert Wendell's current crooked deeds. She's also suggested a way to reach him: through his ramrod, Donovan.

For this Cutter figured he owed Emily Vandermeer, but she was dead and burials took time. He tugged the

46

reins and turned the gelding from the ranch yard toward the north and Bitter Wash.

A flaming magenta sunset was upon the land, and the cries of the crushed man on the hill had ceased. Cutter judged he was less than an hour's ride from the town.

He hoped the cafés there had plenty of steak.

Chapter 6

It was full night when the tall, lone horseman entered Bitter Wash. Lamplight from the windows of the town's buildings splashed on wide, level streets, and shouts raised from saloons and stores carried through still-warm air. Somewhere, a tinny piano tinkled. Through doors left open to trap breezes, Cutter studied people as he rode: busy housewives rattling pans in humble residences, aproned merchants in their stores, late patrons availing themselves of barbers' and blacksmiths' services.

Toward the bustling center of things, activity moved into the street. Men in frock coats came and went from a large hotel, conveyances tooled up and down, hilarity rocked drinking places. Through batwing doors on an establishment with a large GAMBLING sign, a man in puncher's clothes hurtled. He stumbled, fell headlong, and his hat rolled in the dirt. A brawl broke out in a bordello called Roxie's, involving women clad in diaphanous wraps. The Lone Star saloon housed a tableau: two brawny gents in shirtsleeves squared off with fists raised. Then raucous laughter shook them, and they turned back and downed their whiskey.

The lights, noise and tawdriness of the town disgusted Cutter, who had known this same ground in former times. When it had been his pa's ranch—the Circle C—peace and beauty draped these heights and flats. Cattle had grazed rich range, and the night's quiet was broken only by low coyote cries. But tonight Cutter's most baleful glare went to the mansion on the hill, the one whose lights could be seen from all over Bitter Wash. This was Bert Wendell's guarded fortlike house, according to the Vandermeer woman.

A livery barn huddled between a café and a shop that sold ladies' hats, and Cutter directed his weary mount toward it. At the entrance that reeked of hay and manure he called: "Hello, the stable! Anybody home?"

"Hell, yes!"

"Boarding horses tonight?"

"Six bits for a stall, two bits for oats!"

The big man stepped from leather, eased his Winchester from the boot and canted it on his shoulder. He handed the reins to the old-timer who hobbled up. "The animal's had a long, hard trip. Treat him to the best."

The geezer's expression turned sly. "You want to spend a whole dollar on him? For a good rubdown and a blanket?"

Cutter scowled. "Rubdown's part of board."

"T'aint!"

The tall, broad bulk of the big man crowded the geezer into a corner between piled bales. Here the light from the rafter-hung lantern was much more dim. Here the men couldn't be spied clearly from outside. Worry for his safety started to gnaw the old chiseler. The grizzled sideburns twitched with anxiety. The liver-spotted hands shook as he raised them with

49

their palms out.

"Don't mean no harm, mister. Just tryin' to get along."

"Cheating travelers?"

"Cheat ever'body I can, th' locals, too. All fools get th' same treatment."

Cutter backed away and the tension eased. "The bay gets the best you got, but the charge'll be regular. Now, how's the hotel in this town?"

"All right, I reckon."

"I'll check it. Café?"

A brusque "ahem" rose in the old man's throat. "For eats, or for palaver?" He raised his arm as if to point, and a disgusting odor of the unwashed drifted from him.

"Eats."

"Try next door, then."

"If the steak turns out tasteless, fella, I take the price out of your hide."

Not only was the steak tolerable, but side dishes of turnips and calf's-head soup were the same. Cutter passed up prairie oysters because calf-gelding season was months past and he didn't trust the product. His only complaint was that the coffee was weak and cool.

He sat at the tiny table and stared at empty plates. Then the hard eyes roamed across the café's dining room. He'd been aware the place was emptying and that the hour was late. Now the only other person in view was the buxom waitress with the fat, slack face. Voluptuous attractiveness had departed her years ago, leaving a solid woman, overweight and looking like hell. She waddled near, her tight dress threatening to split. "Can I get you anything else, mister?"

He used a hand to scrub a stubbled cheek. "No more food. Got a question you might answer."

She primped henna-orange hair. "My name's Myrt. The owner'll let me off if I ask. Gents give me two dollars for a toss in the hay."

"You ain't worth it."

She turned to go.

"Hold on!" Cutter snapped. "About a fella named Max Donovan. Where can I find him?" He was about to lay down a dollar tip for the woman, but her features went pale and she stood open-mouthed.

The big man quickly rose from the chair. "My guess is that you know the gent, gal."

"I don't know nothing, mister."

He thought he was making it easy for her, earning money without getting on her back. But she spun on her run-down heel and broke from him, scuttling toward the kitchen. She went through the door and slammed it, but he yanked it open and plunged through.

A sideburn-sandwiched face scowled and an enormous belly thrust to block Cutter's way. Between a cookstove and a table of stacked dishes the woman cowered. She'd told her troubles to the cook, and now he went at Cutter, swinging a skillet.

Cutter ducked; the cast-iron handle dented the wall and loosed a tide of hanging utensils. Flapjack-turners raced flour-sifters and giant spoons to crash noisily to the floor.

He launched a fist to the round midsection, burying his arm to the wrist. Then he powered an uppercut to

51

the protruding lip, flinging the cook's head back and knocking off his cap. The cook slammed into the stove and sent pots of liquid splashing. Great gushes of steam burst from the hot surface as the man howled.

"Jesus, Chester, I'm clearin' out," Myrt the waitress squealed.

Cutter disagreed, diving at her and bringing her up short. He'd wrapped his hand in the front of her dress and hauled her close. "Donovan, Myrt! Where?"

"Damn you, stranger! Don't you know it means my hide to finger the collectin' son of a bitch!"

"Wha—" Cutter began. But he saw the look in her eye and spun quickly. The greasy Chester had grabbed up a meat axe and charged. The three people were hemmed into close quarters, and there was no room for Cutter to dodge.

He dipped his shoulder under the slashing blade, which thudded into the doorjamb and stuck, quivering. Then, powering with his elbow, Cutter drove into the cook's chin. The skin of the cook flushed bright purple as he hinged over into the counter.

The counter gave way. An eruption of sound—breaking dishes—overwhelmed Chester's curses. With lightning speed Cutter closed in and pinned the cook against the wall with his big Bowie.

"Now, Chester, if that's your handle—"

"Yeah, it is."

Cutter flourished the knife. "I get the feeling my question about Donovan scares you and the gal. Like the jasper's got some hold on folks in town."

Two round heads bobbed clownishly.

" 'Collecting son of a bitch,' was what Myrt called him." Cutter's face loomed close to the cook's, menace behind the sooty stubble, more blood in the eyes. "Want to know my guess? Donovan takes a fee from stores and such in Bitter Wash. The owner that don't pay, he gets burned out or worse."

Myrt and Chester exchanged looks.

Cutter pressed on relentlessly. "Donovan ain't alone in it. If I take him out, he'll be replaced. And anybody found to have helped *me* out, well—" He let the ominous words hang. Then: "Let me make this quick, on account of I'm getting tired."

His strong fingers clutched the blade tightly, and brought it up. The fat Chester was pressed to the wall, Cutter's gaze fixed on Myrt. She bit her lip. The cook's breath hissed harshly in and out.

With deliberate slowness, the knife point descended on Chester's cheek. As the sharp edge pricked skin, droplets of blood oozed. The cook whined like a kicked dog. "I don't want you to think I got it in for you, fella," Cutter bit out. "It's just that I need to know what you know. And why should I coddle someone who tried to chop me up?"

"For Christ's sake, mister," Myrt complained, "ain't you got understanding for folks too weak to fight? The man that controls this town, he's killed people."

Cutter knew that much. "It takes a hard man to stop that kind."

"Oh, Chester, do what he wants!" The woman called Myrt sagged against a half-filled potato bushel. "My boss ain't a bad sort, stranger."

"Donovan, he drinks at a saloon called the Palace."

Cutter sheathed the knife. "Take me there." Anticipating a refusal, he drew his Colt. "I got a reason."

Leaving a fretful Myrt as they exited through the

53

back of the café, Cutter and the cook found themselves in a dark alley cluttered with rain barrels, busted crates and mating cats. Shrill meows played a counterpoint to the men's footfalls as the big man urged the fat man to pick up his pace. "Just a little ways more, mister," Chester wheezed.

"I'm sure."

"It's true. There's the place's back door. See where that drunk fella's pissin' on the wall?"

Cutter had already noted the shadowy figure and his glistening stream. "We'll wait till he goes back in," he said, "and then you'll follow him."

"Me, go in the saloon?" Chester protested. "But—"

"You'll spot Donovan and mosey over to him. Say something that'll send him out back here. Remember, I'm trusting you, Chester, 'cause I need to stay out of the Palace myself. Don't want no showdown in front of witnesses, savvy?"

"Yeah."

"Gent's going in now, so get on after him."

Chester waddled across the pool of lamplight and inside, where he disappeared behind a stack of beer kegs. Cutter lost no time holstering his sixgun and legging it along the side of the building toward Main Street. The lanterns slung from poles along the thoroughfare gave a low light, and the big man could see clearly the steady flow of tough drifters moving from dive to dive. Cowpunchers either staggered past drunk or strode past sober. Glitter gals sashayed with gents in tow. Gamblers in frock coats twirled canes that could have been rigged with hideout derringers.

A good many *hombres* wore the unmistakable stamp of gunfighter, their hands casually held near low-slung sixguns, beady eyes watchful and never still.

And then one more hardcase joined the strolling outfit. Through the Palace's varnished batwings Max Donovan stepped. Lamplight shone on the stocky man's black vest.

Cutter knew him immediately as the jasper from the pond, the one the Vandermeer woman had hated for taking vile advantage. The hate that had mushroomed when she'd found her brothers dead and herself betrayed. Tonight in the busy street Donovan showed no guilt. In fact, he might have been celebrating. He carried the bottle of Taos rotgut booze he'd been swilling at the bar. But Donovan swaggered rather than staggered, which meant the ramrod held his liquor well.

Cutter joined him on the boardwalk. "Have a few words, mister? I hear Bert Wendell don't cotton to callers, the uninvited kind. But you can get me in to see your boss. It's important."

Donovan stared angrily. "What the goddamn hell — ?"

"*This* important." Cutter thumbed the breech on the cutlass pepperbox that he'd palmed, and the retractable blade extended, jabbing Donovan's ribs. "Now," he bit out, "let's amble easy-like up the street toward the mansion on the hill. If the boss ain't up this late, we'll just wake him."

"*Hombre,* you're loco to be tryin' this." Donovan's voice was gruff. "But, by God, I ain't sorry for what's goin' to happen next."

"I said —"

Cutter was interrupted. His sidelong vision told him Chester was approaching at a fast waddle. Perhaps bringing a warning to him. Out of the corner of his

55

mouth he grated: "Yeah, Chester? Did this varmint tip his pards?"

"That ain't all," the cook with the huge belly rasped. He fetched a stout arm around with surprising speed, and Cutter glimpsed a flashing knife.

Donovan dove away and clawed at his sixgun.

"Blast the stranger, boys!" he roared. "Give the big bastard a hideful of lead—now!"

Chapter 7

Muzzle flashes erupted from under the porch roof of the Palace, and hot lead sang. Cutter pumped a kick to Chester's come-together, hinging him over. At the same, he grabbed Donovan and crawfished, hauling the hardcase down.

The pair hove up behind a brimful horse trough. "Call off your dogs, mister."

"Screw you!"

The gunsels threw more shots, missing Cutter, piercing the trough . . . and Chester, who hadn't moved fast enough to dodge. The cook twitched grotesquely as the slugs made impact with his paunch and throat. Blood flooded the bespattered apron, mingling with smeared griddle grease. Finally the café-owner fell, dead when he hit the street.

With hot lead still winging, Cutter tried Donovan a last time. "You could swing for those Vandermeer killings. All I got to do is tip off the law."

"Not in this town, big man!"

Max Donovan wasn't merely a bad man, he was a stubborn one. Cutter clenched his teeth and moved. Wet from sloshed trough water, he powered up, shielding himself with the struggling Wendell henchman. Instantly Donovan took a slug in the chest and slumped over. Cutter plucked up the heavy body like a shield, and ran toward the pair of shootists. As soon as he reached the boardwalk, he heaved Donovan. One killer reeled back, struck by the flying, flailing form. The other turned and ran.

Cutter tossed a shot, and the man threw up his arms and veered into a hitchrail. The rigid crossbar hit his midsection violently, so that he somersaulted and fell hard at the hooves of a surprised horse.

"You killed this one too, stranger!"

A lawman with a brass star—whom Cutter had never laid eyes on before—knelt beside the victim the Donovan corpse had downed. And it was true that the flattened man's skull looked cracked, resting on a stone doorstep of a photographer's shop. The badge-packer quickly straightened up, brushing off his pants and glaring at Cutter.

"Looked like self-defense to me, Sheriff Quade." The drummer in the threadbare suit of worsted spoke up boldly. Now the bystanders who'd fled to alleys and doorways were reappearing and drifting across the street. Several more nodded solemnly in the big man's behalf.

"That varmint and that 'un," croaked a relic with a cueball pate. "They just pulled their shootin' irons and cut loose."

"Shocking."

"True, they couldn't hit a barn."

A monte thrower in a green eyeshade agreed. "The big jasper had a million-in-one chance, but he cashed the gunsels in!" He was paying off a bet to a grinning companion.

Cutter, his expression unreadable and grim, holstered his weapon. "There ain't no charges to be brought, Sheriff. Reckon I'll just be moseying."

"Wait! Max Donovan, he was my friend!"

"Somebody as'd call *him* one—" Cutter paused and shrugged.

Sheriff Quade's scowl was stormy. "Say, stranger, what did you say your name was?"

Cutter, who'd rocked in a saddle through a long and tiring day, yawned nonchalantly.

"Awright, don't you say nothin'," Quade grouched. "You likely only tell lies, anyways. We're used to such drifters as you, here in Bitter Wash. Saddle tramps and bounty hunters. Grub-line trash anglin' for handouts." He spat a slimy globule of saliva that the ground soaked up.

As he listened, Cutter's view of the town became clear. Bert Wendell's bailiwick deserved contempt, but there was more reason for it than he'd first understood. It was a place that both lured and spawned riffraff, with which it by now was crammed. Newcomers were presumed troublemakers because the town itself was trouble.

"Sheriff, I ain't a broke grub-line beggar, and I can pay my way handsome, if there's call to. That ought to give me as many rights as anybody. I aim to spend the night in your town, and stay as long as I please. Now I'll say good night to you. Better wake the undertaker's men to pick up the garbage."

He turned his back on Quade and the murmuring crowd standing outside the Palace. A short walk put the big man at the hotel, a two-story structure with a false front, a sagging verandah and a faded sign announcing the name: Sunflower House. But before he

59

was able to mount the steps, a female form darted from the shadows and stood in his path. Cutter recognized the waitress from the café.

"You son of a bitch," Myrt blurted.

"Ma'am, it's been a long day."

Her eyes were dark from pain as well as the sooty kohl makeup that tears had smudged. "You mean 'long,' mister, like the rest of my life is gonna be without Chester? True, he worked me waiting tables all day, pimped me at night, but he was my man, and I allus had him. What've I got now? Burial expenses I can't afford! And all because you ate a steak, but didn't think you got enough for your money. You wanted information besides."

He moved to get past her.

"No, you won't take any blame. It figures. You're like all the rest."

"Speaking of rest, lady, don't we both need some?"

Brushing past, leaving the woman perplexed, he walked inside. "Room," he told a pimply-faced youth behind the desk.

The kid rose grudgingly from his stool and rubbed his eyes. "Number twenty, second floor in the rear. That be all right for suitin' you, mister?"

"Well, it ain't all wrong."

The big man exchanged money for a bent and tarnished key and trudged upstairs. Number twenty was no more than twelve feet square, low-ceilinged, with peeling wallpaper. The face he glimpsed in the chipped washstand mirror, he simply ignored. He was trail-dirty and unshaven. His hair was lank. He hung his Stetson on a peg, and his gunbelt on the bedpost with the butt toward the pillow. The bed sagged under his massive bulk, but at least it was a bed.

He dozed fully clothed.

His dreams were based on old memories.

The hills and swales on which the town of Bitter Wash had sprung toadstool-like were again open range. Brush-choked draws cut the terrain crookedly, and the creek flanked by cottonwoods wound through grass that was tall and green. Outside a pole-raftered house a lanky boy worked at splitting firewood. The chore made him sweat, but happily.

A tall man appeared in the doorway and called out. "Jeb, son! Supper! I'm about to sit at table and ask the Lord's blessing on us!"

The boy dropped off the axe in a shed, ran inside and took his place at the homemade table. The food wasn't fancy, but it was plentiful: boiled beef and bannock. And a dessert made of preserved peaches out of an airtight jar. The lad grinned a lot at his father, and Enoch Cutter smiled back. Over the Bible stand in the room's corner hung a tintype of a dark-haired, pretty young woman. The picture was all Jeb had ever known of his ma, and it was precious to both father and son.

The dream turned fitful.

It was the next day. They were on the small spread's outer range for calf-gather, the father and the son. A warm spring sun beat down. Dust filled the air, and there were dozens of bawling calves. Enoch and Jeb sweated heavily over the fire that kept the branding iron hot.

61

The dream skipped ahead. Now Enoch Cutter lay dead. The branding iron was searing flesh—Jeb's flesh—and a smelly smoke puff wafted away. The pain on the youth's chest seemed beyond belief. Screams rang out, and the screams were the young man's own. There was laughter from the roughneck raiders . . . and in addition from a deep, cultured, Alabama drawl, that of ranchman Bert Wendell. Wendell stood beside Ike Hines, both enjoying the kid's suffering.

Rays of morning sunshine shafted through fly-specked windowpanes, and a breeze smelling of back-alley garbage piles stirred hole-laced curtains. The sound that had yanked the big man from his restless sleep was repeated, louder this time.

Knuckles were rapping insistently on the door.

Cutter filled his big hand with his Colt, uncoiled from the bed, and, catlike, edged along the wall. He drew the bolt of the door back abruptly, turned the latch and jerked open the panel. On the threshold stood a man in a black frock coat and clipped goatee, and Cutter swiftly hauled him in. The stranger's dove-gray vest took most of the punishment from the gripping fist, unless you counted the beaver hat that rolled on the floor and was stamped by the big man.

"Speak your piece fast, fella," Cutter hissed. "I ain't in a real good mood."

The gent spoke around an unlit, crooked stogie. "Well, Jowett is my name and gambling is my game," he said easily. "Hollis Jowett, that is." He showed a lopsided grin. "The gambling comes with running my saloon, the Silver Horseshoe. You don't know me," he assured the man with a hand on his throat, "but I've heard of your doings of last night, as has most of the town."

Cutter's distrustful eyes slitted.

"I've come to tell you about a gent called Wendell."

Chapter 8

The sun shone as brightly upon the mansion on the hilltop overlooking Bitter Wash as it did in the lower town, and the walls with many windows basked in morning light. The beams through glass flung yellow rectangles across an interior furnished in fine mahogany, making the chairs and other parlor pieces shine. Pier glass mirrors reflected burled paneling and chandeliers from France. Damask draperies hung in scarlet folds.

Three varnished coffins on brass stands glinted somberly in the parlor's center, the ebony wood set off richly by silver handles and facings. Yawning lids showed off the contents: the corpses of Max Donovan and his pards, who'd been ugly in life, and remained so despite the mortician's craft.

The wake would last through the morning hours. Burial was set for noon, at which time the undertaker's hearse was expected to arrive to make the trip to the cemetery. Meanwhile, it was quiet in the mansion, the loudest sound the low buzz of flies.

The air inside the parlor was oppressive, the stench of decomposing flesh strong as a physical blow. Vases of flowers did little for the atmosphere. Uncorked vapor salts did less.

In a deep upholstered chair of fine cordovan, the sole live inhabitant of the room sat with features screwed tight in a mask. He was a cadaverous man of middle age, his face set in a perpetual scowl. A nervous tic worked in one cheek hollow, setting a gray longhorn mustache to twitching. The light, white suit the man wore was damp with sweat spots, but he made no move—either to fan himself or flee from the stink. The carved briar pipe in his fingers had gone out, but not the blaze in the eyes.

He slapped a hand on the chair arm vigorously, and a man in a linen servant's jacket hurried in. Bowing, the fawning fellow said, "Mr. Wendell, yessir?"

"Snap to it, Jim, boy, when I want you! Now about Frank Gideon. Is the man in the house?"

"You bet he is!"

Bert Wendell's top bodyguard was never far from his chief. And with Max Donovan dead, the tough man was going to be counted on more and more. "Send him in here to me."

Jim tugged at his collar. "Right away, boss." He went out like a scuttling rat.

Minutes dragged by. Then rasping words preceded a loud-voiced speaker into the room. "Christ, boss, you sittin' with the stiffs? What in hell for?" The man who entered was rawboned and whipcord-rugged, his face pocked, and browned by years lived in the outdoors. A Dakota-creased hat rode his brow. Tied-down holsters rode his hips.

He moved well for a man extremely bowlegged. He stopped, fixed by Bert Wendell's stare. "Er—But I ain't sayin' it ain't your right. You're the boss. Sittin' with stiffs just could have a use."

Wendell scowled into the eyes of tough Frank Gideon. "Seein' Donovan and the Dibbs cousins, it riles me," the older man growled. "Being my distant kin like they was, and crack shots—then, poof! They're gone!" The eyes turned to squeezed-narrow slits. "The boys done questionin' the folks that was in the street last night?"

A crisp nod. "Appears Max and the Dibbs cousins tangled with a stranger outside the Palace. A damned tough-nut stranger."

"I want the reason for what happened. And I want the son-of-a-bitchin' stranger dead!"

Wendell's cheek tic had become more noticeable, a fact not lost on the hardcase. Still, Gideon could do little but shrug. "Oh, he'll be gettin' his. Y'know, seems nobody in town seen him before the shootin' started. 'Cept, it's said, for Chester, and Chester's killed now, too."

Wendell hauled to his feet, stiffly. "Damned mess." Nearer the coffins he found the smell worse. "Maybe we *had* better stroll a mite outside." The man in the white suit led the way. Down a hallway hung with paintings Wendell and Gideon strode, emerging at last at the rear of the huge house. An enormous live oak cast shade on the yard, and the men paused in it. Across a flagstone terrace were the edge of the bluff and a drop-off. Below lay the town.

"Chester. That's the Chester that ran the café? Paid his protection money to us regular?"

Gideon confirmed it. "Onliest Chester there was in Bitter Wash."

"Oh, ye-es." Wendell's drawl of the eastern South

66

told of his origins. Not a Texan born, but he'd arrived, a newcomer, about thirteen years before. He'd inherited some family money made on a cotton plantation, but not an extremely large sum, and carried a determination to grow rich in ranching. Become a cattle baron.

The goal could be achieved in those years by stealing the land of small fry.

Such had been Bert Wendell's secret of success.

Now, on the hill that held his mansion and its luxuries, he surveyed the town he'd built and now owned. It was income without much work anymore, except for henchmen's toil. But last night, in front of the Palace, he'd lost three of those henchmen, including his valued segundo.

The sour fact had curtailed Wendell's glee about the Vandermeers' deaths. Elimination of the brothers gave him another foreclosure, a good development. But the loss of Max Donovan wasn't so good.

The tic recurred along Wendell's lean jaw.

He spoke now with a low-pitched hiss. "Donovan's job, Gideon. You figure you can handle it?"

The hardcase's face broke into something like a smile. "Mr. Wendell, I'd be proud to try my best." His palm scrubbed his chin. "Wringin' money outa scared little folks. Playin' with 'em if they don't pay their dues. Seein' 'em sweat blood, and seein' 'em change their minds." A laugh. "My style, boss. Just my style."

"Let's drink to it." Bert Wendell raised his voice in a loud call. "Hey, Jim!"

The little man appeared in the doorway.

"A couple of juleps, Jim—Say! Somethin' wrong?"

The servant gulped. "A fella's here. I rec'gnize him; he's the barber from the town. Come to the door ravin' how his payment ain't gonna get made. How he give his money to the doc, on account of his wife's sick —"

A short, frail man in a candycane-striped shirt appeared behind Jim, pomaded hair showing a straight, neat part, but his round face showing decided strain. "I come to tell you face-to-face, Mr. Wendell. How it stands is this way —"

Wendell's scowl stayed, but his color purpled with deeper anger. "What the hell? Get a couple of the boys out here!" Then to the visitor: "I know you, Craig Luke! You give good shaves, but you're a staller when comes time to pay dues! You've taken your bruises for this kind of play before! And you've the gall to come here today?"

"My Etta, she's been feelin' so poorly —"

"Bullshit!"

Not two, but three burly hardcases with their six-guns out came through the door. The trio surrounded skinny Craig Luke, who peered about in fear. "Throw him out, boss?" a gunsel with one whitish eye growled. "Roughin' him up a bit on the way?"

"You read my mind, Squint. Teach him a lesson — No, wait!" Wendell sneered, the mustache lifting. "Now could be the chance for a timely test. Frank Gideon, come here."

Gideon stepped to his boss's side.

"I reckon I know what to do, Mr. Wendell." He glared at the barber, who'd begun to quake. It had seemed to him a good idea back in the shop, making explanation how the money "owed" was gone — but

68

that his wife was doing better on the new medicine. How starting next month he'd be able to again make his regular payments. . . .

But Wendell was talking again. "Luke, your duty's like every tradesman's duty in this town. Pay up, and make no excuses. No short changin'. I let one jasper slide, that's a bad example set. You folks're buyin' protection from harm. Like what's about to strike you down now!"

"But, Mr. Wendell, sir—"

"Frank Gideon," Wendell interrupted. "I want you to outdo the late Max Donovan's style, if you can. Make an example of Mr. Luke here."

"Too bad for this sucker," Gideon gloated, drawing on scuffed rawhide gloves. Without more warning, he drove his fist into Craig Luke's solar plexus. The little man doubled over, purpled, spewed vomit down his chin and onto the freshly ironed shirt.

Then Gideon's knee came up sharply to Luke's mouth, slamming him back and against the tree. "You threw up on my pants! I'll make you pay!" He waded in with flurrying lefts and rights, battering the round head, snapping it back and forth, pendulumlike.

Frank Gideon stomped the victim's flimsily shod foot, and Bert Wendell smiled approval—a wicked smile. "I won't break your arm," Frank Gideon snapped, " 'cause then you couldn't cut hair so good." He spun Luke around roughly, then dealt kidney punches with tough-gloved fists. Bursts of pain shot along Luke's ribcage and up his spine. The man saw stars behind his squeezed eyelids. He went down on the ground, rolling, and became a target for brutal kicks.

Five minutes later, after the boot toes had wrought dire damage, Craig Luke was barely conscious. He was still bleeding from his mouth, and several ribs were cracked. In the beating only his hands had been spared . . . and one other area. Then Gideon's voice rang out, deep and clear. "Drag down the fella's britches!"

No! Craig Luke raged inwardly. *No! This I can't stand! I know I can't!*

But despite weak attempts at struggling, soon the breeze wafted over the barber's shriveled parts. He popped his eyes open and glimpsed a razor clutched by Gideon.

Craig Luke fainted away.

"Shucks, I wasn't gonna geld him. Just scare him, so's he'd pay what he owes after this."

"I don't think we'll have any more trouble from the young barber." Bert Wendell ran a hand over his smooth dome. "Nice work. Now, shall we celebrate with those juleps?"

"Would taste mighty good on such a hot day, boss."

Wendell barked at the gunsels: "Take this scum home in a fodder wagon, toss him out in front of his door. No need to bother with the wife — this time."

"So you see," Hollis Jowett said conversationally, "now I've told you the deals Bert Wendell pulls, you're going to want to throw in with me."

Cutter, beside the bed, glared at his visitor with smoldering eyes.

The gambler was pale-skinned in the way of men

70

who live by night, and the darkish sorrel Van Dyke beard contrasted with the pasty face. The frock coat hung over hunched, narrow shoulders, and the bones stood out on his hands, along with the spiderings of blue veins. Now Jowett tugged out a snowy kerchief, coughed and spat in it, and Cutter glimpsed blood flecks.

"Well, then, Mr. — er — ?"

"Name's Cutter. But ain't no cause to broadcast it."

"Hell, I ain't inclined." Jowett stuffed the soiled hanky in his hip pocket, the one that held no derringer. "Now you know Wendell practically runs the town, takin' ten percent off the businesses, collecting most building rents. Not much ranchland in the area he hasn't grabbed up over the years. Controls the bank through the banker. Keeps an army of paid gunsels on his payroll. I've given you the general layout, Cutter, and a raft of details besides. I'm about the lone holdout against the tyrant, and I'm ready to declare war."

Cutter dug the makings from his slept-in clothes. His chin had another day's growth of stubble. He'd been up late, and he'd been wakened early. His mood was a trifle worse than usual. "You want me to sign on your gunfighter crew, account of what I showed I could do last night."

"You took out three of Wendell's best."

"For my own reasons, mister. As to your offer, Jowett, no soap."

"You're a loner, hey? Let me mention the figure I aim to pay a top gun — "

The quirly rolled, Cutter repocketed the muslin sack of Dixie Queen. The match he scratched on his

71

grubby thumbnail flared, and he bent his shaggy head to light up. The big man sucked a lungful of smoke and exhaled. Jowett coughed and clamped teeth in his unlit cigar. "Ain't interested."

"Whatever you say." A shrug. "But if you figure you'll make a loner play in Bitter Wash, look out—"

Cutter drew the Colt from its holster. He didn't look at the consumptive gambler, merely eared the hammer of his weapon with a click.

Jowett regarded Cutter, seeing him as the truly mean customer that he was. A shudder shook the gambler's bones. "All right, mister. I'm gone."

Jowett eased the door shut after him.

Cutter puffed his quirly and scratched his chest, but didn't put the gun away. He was squinting into the clouded mirror above the washstand and saw the reflection of a tall Texas hat edging above the windowsill. A head and body followed, with two hands gripping a Greener twelve-gauge. The big man saw ladder rails nudge grimy glass. The shotgunner was positioning himself.

Cutter's hand swept up the water pitcher and flung it, the window shattering simultaneously at the attacker's blow. The scattergun discharged with a roar, and a cloud of buckshot hurtled.

Chapter 9

A hot blast of flame cut the room's resounding air, spearing past Cutter just as the big man dropped flat. Flying pellets grazed the diving man's skin. Trickles of blood sluiced Cutter's neckerchief as most of the charge rushed past. The mattress behind him erupted in an explosion of horse hair.

Cutter powered up, grabbed the Greener's double barrels, and jerked mightily to drag over the sill both gun and wielder. Broken glass showered; the gunman crashed in and to the floor. Cutter stamped on the jasper's hands, kicking the shotgun from them. He snatched the weapon up and swung it hard across the face. There was the crackle of breaking cheekbone and the man pitched backward. The screaming mouth fountained gore as the owner's shoulder blades slammed the bedpost.

But the jasper rebounded. Caroming off the bedstead with his arms windmilling, he charged Cutter, not a particularly large man himself, but game.

Cutter sidestepped, tripped the man, and fell on him knees first, driving the wind from him. The big man still gripped the fired Greener. He brought the stock down across the owner's forehead, the sharp buttplate slicing down to skin, flesh and bone.

73

The jasper's eyes bulged with his pain; his hand flew to his face. Blood trickled through the clasped fingers.

And then he pulled his hands away, lurched up on stumpy legs and charged.

The two men met in the middle of the floor and Cutter felt himself pushed back. Between the bed and the low-standing commode there was no room to swing the Greener. He dropped it and began throwing punches, sledge blows to the other's chest, arms, face. Then the man dropped his head and bulled into Cutter, a solid impact with his chest. Breath hissed through Cutter's teeth as he gasped with pain.

He was being bear-hugged and couldn't breathe; pain-wracked seconds ticked off as he struggled against the jasper's lucky grip. Blackness rose in the big man's brain, but he fought on, twisting in his foe's clutches, grappling with fingers set like hooks. With an enormous heave he planted thumbs in the jasper's throat, grinding down hard into the voice box. Abruptly the vise lock broke, and Cutter propelled the wiry man back. He held onto an arm and, hauling him in, broke it across the bedstead with a brittle snap.

"Christ, he busted me! Billy! Blast the son of a bitch!"

Cutter spun and saw the other hardcase who'd mounted the ladder, and the leveled sixgun he thrust across the windowsill. In a second he was at the window and shoving powerfully. The tall ladder toppled to the side, man still aboard, and slammed twelve feet to the ground, lofting clouds of alley dust. The would-be sixgunner landed across a fire barrel below.

Cutter swung back to face the man inside.

Bloody-faced and squinting, he crouched in a corner. He hugged his useless right arm in his left, and cried his pain out in low, long moans. The big man crossed to him, jerked him by his shirtfront and thrust his stubbled face near. The coal-chip eyes burned into the man.

"Who wants me dead?" Cutter demanded in an icy voice. "I don't mean you, mister. I mean the bastard who paid you for your dumb play."

"K-kill me! I w-won't tell you nothing!"

"I'll bet. Figure you're tough? Tough like Donovan?"

"Y-you knew Max? Er—I mean—"

Cutter grabbed the man's hair, slammed his head into the wall. "You told me all I need. Well, I'm going to let you live, 'cause it's less trouble than killing you. Go back to your boss or clear out of town, spilling information or else run. Only one thing more I got to do."

The wiry man slunk forward. "What's that? Jesus, you already busted me all up."

"You brought me trouble, and I always pay trouble back. You like to play with guns too much for your good. I aim to cure the habit."

Two-Toes quailed under the killer look. "What you gonna do? Christ! Not my other arm! No, mister! *No!*"

Cutter grabbed the man's fingers as if for a handshake, but brought his strength to bear. He pried back on the digit favored for trigger-stroking; then he followed through and broke that bone too, the levering motion quick and abrupt.

The broken man mewed like a kitten this time, and collapsed. Cutter dragged him to the window, hinged his form across the ledge . . .

And released his hold. The man plummeted to earth like a stone, and hit the alley floor with a thud.

Cutter didn't take time to look out, but heard the pair below cursing vilely and hauling themselves off.

In the same mirror that had shown him his attacker he inspected the scrapes on his neck. No shotgun pellets had lodged in the flesh, but his bandanna was blood-browned and growing stiff. He unknotted it, dabbed himself, and threw the ruined piece of cloth away.

His appetite by now growling in his gullet, Cutter jammed his Stetson on his head and stalked out and down the stairs. At a questioning look from the desk clerk he said, "I'll be checking out later in the day. Have my bill ready."

"Isn't the room comfortable?"

"Glass on the floor. Ain't safe to walk."

Stepping outside, he thought of breakfast at Chester's, recalled Chester was dead. Decided Myrt's service mightn't be offered with much of a smile this morning.

Cutter turned his strides up the street.

He passed the newspaper office and the noisy crowd rapidly gathering in front.

"Damn! Looka this!"

"Editor Tomlinson, he's did it again! A reg'lar scoop!"

76

"You b'lieve that headline? 'Redskins Raid Ranch, Kill Vandermeer Family'?" Excitement rode the people's faces as Cutter strode up.

Now the shouter was a prune-faced, mat-haired hag. "Gotta b'lieve it! Ain't it in print?"

"Damn them renegade bucks from up the Indian Nation way! Raidin' again after broncs and fire-water!"

Cutter's gaze sized up the bunch as typical frontier dwellers, filled with ghoulish interest over a gruesome incident. Except for a particular young man standing subdued at the edge of things. His unusual appearance set him apart, especially his clothes, which were uniquely Eastern. His slim build was decked in a shirt of downy flannel, plus twill riding britches of a kind Cutter had seen only in picture books. A stiff sun helmet rode the dude's head.

His handsome features carried an expression of deep grief.

As Cutter approached, the stiff-pants gent told a townsman; "My poor, dear Emily. Yesterday morning so vital, full of life. Today, dead. If I'd only insisted she accompany me instead of go alone for her infernal horseback ride—"

"And what'd you be doin' yestiday, sonny?" inquired the old-timer.

"I took my brushes and paints to Diablo Canyon for—"

"Tenderfoot tomfoolery?"

"Huh!" the Easterner snorted. "Why, for capturing on canvas a magnificent countryside! Art is my life, my man! Painting the glories of the wondrous West!

77

Make the name Cyril Wilkes famous that way! It was my ambition for my fiancée's sake!"

So the fellow Wilkes had been sweet on the gal, Cutter noted, plunging past and shouldering through toward the newspaper-office door. He wondered idly about the dude's opinion if he'd known the woman hadn't *merely* taken a horseback ride. That she'd given herself to Max Donovan, hoping to save her brothers' lives. That the whole intrigue had misfired miserably.

And that the three Vandermeers had been gunned down by Bert Wendell's men.

Since all the fallout of Wendell's land grab wasn't his concern, Cutter wanted to read the paper for other reasons. To see if his name had appeared as a result of last night's shootout. He wasn't sure whether he'd been recognized—he'd been jailed in the Texas panhandle region quite a few years before. He was doubtful his changed face would be remembered hereabouts. Ike Hines hadn't known it.

Hines had recognized the brand on his chest when he'd been shown. Now, for his knowledge about the disfigurement, Hines lay buried in the boot hill of the town of Pecos.

To Cutter's way of thinking, the scum deserved company in death.

And so now he pushed past Emily's painter friend. "Damn it! Let me through!" he growled to the crowd. Those who turned and saw him cringed and made way. The big man oozed cruelty.

Finally he stood on the doorstep beneath the large sign: BITTER WASH TRIBUNE. There he locked eyes with a rotund individual, dapper in checked

78

city pants, pencil behind his ear, starched shirt covered with ink smudges. He spoke in a reedy whine, Western enough, but not Texas. "Sorry, mister," he bleated, "the edition's been sold out. We go to press again a week from today. As of now the office is closed as I adjourn to the saloon to wash the dust down."

"Trail dust?"

"Paper dust. Can play the very devil with a publisher's throat."

He moved to brush past Cutter, but the big man blocked him. "I reckon you're Tomlinson?"

"Clay Tomlinson, yeah. Now, if you'll excuse me, I'm in a rush."

"You're going back inside with me." Cutter opened the door and forced the fat man back through it. The cannonball paunch of the publisher rose and fell with his breaths. "Now," Cutter said, "if I don't read the news, I ain't an informed gent. Not the kind of impression I want to give in Bitter Wash. *Comprende, compadre?*"

"I don't understand Mex talk."

"You savvy common sense?" As he examined his knuckles, the big man put on a show of casualness. However, his clenched fist waved under the nose of Tomlinson, who scurried to his desk.

"I'll let you look at my file copy of the paper. Now, be careful and see it don't get torn."

Cutter scanned the front page, saw the account of the Vandermeer tragedy, which didn't mention the gunsel who'd been crushed by the boulder. The story described the burned building, the way Emily and her brothers had been found dead. The blame

79

was given to Comanche braves, off the reservation. The story announced a quiet funeral slated for the next day.

"Why ain't you upset over a redskin scare?" Cutter asked.

"Why, most of the Injuns are long gone by now. Seems they been known to come raidin' every few years in these parts. Hit, then run like the devil."

"Who found out what happened at the Spade 8 spread?"

Tomlinson hesitated. "Squint Duran came to me with the story. Told me the little I know. Been a reliable reporter in the past. Mr. Wendell's employee."

"I see." Cutter turned to the inner pages, ignoring news of President Grant in far-off Washington, D.C. Neither did he find of interest advertisements for products to cure "females' ills." Peacemaker Colts were selling for fourteen dollars at a local store.

There was nothing in that day's *Tribune* about last night's street shootout. Cutter tossed the paper down.

Clay Tomlinson had edged well across the room from the big man. The publisher's eyes were sly. He held his arm behind a printing press set close to the wall. "What you up to there, newspaperman?" Cutter wanted to know. "Not some dumb-ass trick you aim to play?"

"Er—"

"Show both your hands!"

Grudgingly, the glared-at man brought his hands into view. The right was clenched around a two-foot steel rod, some sort of printer's tool. "Shit, mister,"

Tomlinson rasped, "you barged your ass in here without a by-your-leave. I only aimed to protect myself. Hell, I let you read the news columns, didn't I?"

"You weren't all that polite about it."

"You figure *you* were polite?"

"It's a habit of mine, with gents given to sneaky ways. Dish some bad news onto their plates. Teach them lessons."

Clay Tomlinson was trembling. He eyed the big man with the jutting bristled jaw, the ugly welts chewed in his neck, the result of some painful incident. The publisher knew human nature, but he felt he was confronting a wolf, an animal of prey. Not a shred of mercy showed in the stranger's black eyes, tight mouth. Suddenly, a hand plucked the press rod from him and dropped it. Cutter's other hand hauled on his tie, as if pulling in a hooked fish.

"Seems if I hurt your hands," Cutter was hissing, "you'd be out of business setting type. About the same, should bad things happen to your feet. Reporters need to get around. That leaves—"

The big man had produced a derringer with a sharp blade, which he held under Tomlinson's nose. "But you got to sniff out stories, don't you? That lets the nose out. How 'bout an ear?" With a vicious slash, he sliced the man's ear, venting blood that splashed the soiled shirt and mingled with dark ink stains. The publisher gasped and fell into a swivel chair, sick with pain and nausea. But there was nothing he could do against this big man. The big man turned on his heel and walked toward the door.

Tomlinson bit his lip to hold in a scream, fearing the man might return. His eyes fell on the bloody piece of flesh on the desk. *Oh, my God!* Through the window he heard: "Go on in, folks. The man, he's had him an accident."

The publisher hunched in the chair and vomited over the *Tribune* file copy, a yellowish, tapioca-lumpy stream.

Help ran across the threshold in the form of the toothless old-timer and companions. "Jesus, Tomlinson! What happened? That stranger didn't—?"

The publisher pressed a hand to his bleeding head, all thoughts swimming but those picturing the hard big man. "Him? Oh, no trouble with that fella, Ira. J-just a l-little mishap th-that h-happened to—"

Clay Tomlinson passed out cold, and folded to the floor in a heap.

Chapter 10

Cutter slipped through the livery barn's low-jambed side door, coming into dimness that almost blinded him after the sun's glare in the street. He moved slowly while his eyes adjusted, guided by the sounds from up front: shovel work in stalls, the tuneless humming of the hostler. He found his gelding in its stall, saw that its trough was filled with oats and there was a large bucket with fresh water. The animal's coat shone, a sign of thorough, recent currying.

The big man slipped up on the old hostler pitching hay in the aisle, said: "I'll be taking my mount out a spell. Saddle him."

The old-timer jumped six inches. "Jesus, mister, you caught me unawares. Your animal is the—?"

"Bay. The big one."

"Sure. Big like its owner. I'll be gettin' him ready." While the saddling went on, Cutter lounged in the doorway, surveyed the mansion on the overlooking hill, and the steep road leading from it. His eyes were keen as well as cruel, and as he watched he saw a rig begin the descent, a black four-wheeled conveyance drawn by paired black horses. Black ostrich feathers plumed the bridles of the team.

A hearse.

Five minutes later Cutter rode out into the full bright of day, past the Palace Saloon, in front of the café that had been run by the fat cook Chester. All appeared calm in the town as quiet citizens made their way up and down the boardwalks. The big man was about to knee his mount in the direction of the cemetery, but at that moment a shouting crazed woman ran into the dusty thoroughfare.

Myrt tore a checked, frilled apron from her waist and waved it on high. Her red hair was mussed as a bird's nest, and her voice was shrill. "I'll see you in hell, you son of a bitch," she caterwauled at Cutter. Men in cattlemen's soiled work clothes backed from her path as she charged past them.

She stopped in front of the gelding and shook her small fist. "You!" she told the bit man. "You're to blame for a good fella's death! And there you sit, tall on a bronc and not one bit ashamed! And what am I left with, mister? Work piled to my ass, with runnin' the café by my lonesome! The kitchen work, the waitressin'! Damn you, stranger! Damn you to hell!" She found the strength to spit.

Cutter reined around her and clapped heels to the bay's sides. The gelding sprang past. "Try hiring help, lady! Dishwashers come cheap."

At the juncture of Main Street and the rutted cemetery road, Cutter sat the bay beneath a tall, shading sycamore. Not expecting much wait, he dragged out the makings and built a hand-roll. A mockingbird called above and a jay squawked in the brush, but all else for yards around was eerily

84

quiet. He thumbed the phosphorus tip of a lucifer and touched the flare-up to the quirly, then exhaled blue smoke and gazed aloft to check the sun's angle.

From around the bend he heard harness creaking and wheels on a slow roll. Soon the hearse and team came into view in mournful parade.

The rig was almost certainly the town's fanciest and most imposing. It rode lower than the average Concord coach, but was as long, and had windows of beveled glass set into varnished sides. Brass rails running the length were buffed and shining, as were rear handholds. Except for metal fittings, the rig was black from tailgate to whiffletrees. Black feather plumes swayed in fixtures at all four corners.

A black-clad gaunt gent in a tall hat held the reins. A seeming twin sat next to him on the box.

Cutter could see through the polished glass the three coffins that had been squeezed onto the bed of the rig. They looked like bathtubs with lids and sidehandles, black in color, and agleam in the rays of midday. The thing that surprised the big man was the lack of people, the absence of a cortege.

As the hearse rolled through the cemetery gate and stopped beside the dug graves, Cutter flung his quirly away and spurred the gelding lightly.

His next stop would be the mansion on the hill.

If a polecat won't leave its hole, you can't bushwhack him, the big man's thoughts ran. *It means you've got to try harder. A passel more effort, maybe, but the same bloody wind-up.*

Halfway up the hill road he veered from it and reined in suddenly. Behind a low granite outcrop Cutter waited for six approaching riders to pass. All had the mean look of hired killers, and wore the weapons of the breed: sixguns holstered on cartridge-crammed shellbelts, well-oiled carbines in waxed saddle boots. As they trotted their mounts townward, the men spoke of liquor, brawls and whores.

None of them had spotted Cutter. He gigged the gelding up a side trail next, angling toward the crest. He stopped when he reached a palisade of logs, planted upright in the ground. They looked as sturdy as an army fort's tall wall.

"Shit!"

What he saw angered him, but the reason he'd come was to make this kind of discovery. Bert Wendell was leery of enemies, just as Cutter had been informed. Considering the kingpin and the town, he likely had legions of foes.

Now Cutter turned in the saddle and surveyed the buildings of Bitter Wash spread below like children's toys. The whole area for miles appeared peaceful. Far out on the flat, cattle grazed singly and in bunches. A few riders traveled the roads. Cutter's eyes picked out one on the Spade 8 trail, notable for mediocre horsemanship. The tenderfoot regalia the fellow wore proclaimed him to be Cyril Wilkes.

But Cutter's gaze didn't linger on distant vistas. Bent on getting at Bert Wendell, he put the bay to following the palisade around the hill. Soon clumps of mesquite and thorny serviceberry made hard going for the horse. Branches tore at the big man's clothes. Thrusting stone outcrops forced detours. At last the rider stepped from leather beside the bleached skeleton of a lightning-riven pine.

It appeared possible to climb the trunk of the

dead tree, once a tall loblolly. A man might drop inside the mansion's fenced-off grounds easily from there.

"Thought the ruckus I spotted was along here someplace," a drawling voice complained. Cutter heard the crash of breaking brush, and scuffling boots treading close by. He froze beside the silvered, dry trunk and drew his Colt, cupping his free hand over the bay's muzzle. In another two seconds the mumbling hardcase stepped into sight.

Pocked of face and burly of build, the jasper hefted a well-used sixgun in his right fist. He moved awkwardly in the shifting shale underfoot, often slipping on dislodged chunks and losing his balance. At the moment, Cutter saw just the one gunsel, although he knew Wendell's men often went in teams. He'd earlier faced a Donovan who'd been backed by sidekicks; then a pair had made a play to take his life through the hotel window.

"Don't talk!" Cutter hissed, getting the drop. He stepped near and raised his run to club the jasper's head. The sound of a shot would attract more guards, he knew, thus spoiling that day's stalk of their vicious boss.

A twig snapping behind him made Cutter whirl to face another foe charging from the woods. He found himself butted in the breastbone, and at the same time his foot slipped. But as he fell he dragged the attacker to the ground, yards downhill. He wrenched the pistol from the gunsel's hand and in the same move dipped to his boottop. Out came the twelve-inch Bowie with the cutlass blade at ready. The attacker had already opened his mouth to bellow.

Cutter opened his throat.

With a lightning-swift slash he drew the blade in an arc under the shelving jaw. The head flopped back as if hinged, revealed a wedge of crimson flesh and a blood tide. Then slit arteries ceased their flow as the man's heart beat to a stop. Cutter didn't wait, but rolled on his back to meet the dive of the other Wendell guard.

The shootist had retrieved his gun to draw a hasty bead. Cutter's drawn-back arm snapped forward, flinging the knife.

The blade speared between the fellow's ribs to bring him down crashing. But he was still strong enough to shout a warning. As he gathered steam to shout, Cutter clapped a palm over his lower face, and pulled the knife up, opening his stomach. The man went limp and slumped facedown. Discharging wastes from his bowels flooded, overpowering the pines' perfume.

Cutter turned away.

The big man's features went sour instead of impassive as he stood pondering for more than a minute. He'd found out plenty on this day's little scout. First, that Wendell's place was a patrolled fort that he'd need a sound plan to broach. Next, that the bastard's army of toughs required whittling down.

"Another time, Wendell," Cutter muttered, retrieving his weapon and wiping the blade in a clump of grass. He sheathed his weapon and felt familiar tightness in the skin of his chest.

All the years after the brutal branding of his hide, Cutter kept feeling the stiffness of muscle—a reminder. Bert Wendell had been the wielder of the ʾt iron that day. Wendell was the man who'd shot down his pa.

Now Cutter picked up the bay's reins and swung into the saddle. The killer eyes under hooded lids flashed their hate for the vicious land-grabber.

"Yeah, Wendell. Another time."

In the mansion suite with the drawn velvet draperies, Bert Wendell sat up in bed. A thin bare arm flung the satin pillows back, and ugly fish-white feet churned the crocheted counterpane. The naked female sharing the roomy four-poster lurched away, startled, large pink-crested breasts a-sway.

Rapping on the door was repeated, urgent and loud. Wendell's bald head wrinkled as he scowled. The soup-strainer mustache bristled. "Who's out there?"

"Frank Gideon, boss. I got news."

Wendell glanced at the woman. She was teenaged, lithe, brunette. But she wore smudges under her eyes, and large, brown bruises covered her belly and her thighs. She peered at her companion with the eyes of a scared doe.

"What kind of news?" Wendell demanded.

"Not good."

"Then come on the hell in!"

Gideon wasn't alone, but trailed by two gunsels who looked just returned from war. One walked with a severe limp, almost dragging himself. The other nursed injured hands and arms swinging at his sides. Both men's faces were screwed taut with pain. "Here's Billy Kydd and Two-toes Joe Mc-Cady," Frank Gideon announced. The bowlegged segundo stood at the foot of the bed, ignoring the girl.

She scooted to the far side of the mattress, swung her legs over and stood up, eyes cast to the floor. She walked to the doorway of the adjoining room, through beaded curtains and on into it. There, out of direct sight, she gave herself to racking sobs.

None of the men paid the least attention.

"They located the stranger in the hotel," Gideon declared. "But they claim he was mean as a bull and tough as an outlaw bronc. It seems he—"

"Spare me the details!" Wendell wrapped his spare frame in a silk robe. "So the son of a bitch adds two more tallies to his score."

Two-Toes and Billy Kydd stared at their old, scuffed boots.

"So where's the son of a bitch now?" Wendell paced to the wallside chiffonier and punched his pipe into his mouth.

"Dunno—"

The boss's hatchet face came around fiercely. "Then, damnit, who does know? I want the stranger skewered and skinned! I want—" A pause. "Wait a minute! That fat grubslinger, Chester, knew the stranger. That hag waitress woman's got to know him too! Fetch the bitch."

"Ask her questions."

"*I'll* ask the questions, damn it, Gideon! You just fetch her here!"

On his and the others' way out, the new segundo leered maliciously. He always liked it when called on to work in the cellar under the mansion. Some of his most enjoyable times had been experienced there.

The things he was picturing doing to Myrt would

have made Craig Luke the barber thank his lucky stars.

Wendell found the bruised brunette huddled in a closet. "Slut! Goddamn tight-ass slut! Hide from me, will you?"

From behind the exotic beaded curtain, a chorus of blows rang out. Then all was quiet but for a violent slap-slap of flesh.

And low, pained whimpering.

Chapter 11

Cutter moved his long legs stiffly as he left the livery after depositing the bay. He hadn't meant to scare the bejesus out of the hostler, but he'd managed to. The carved features of his embittered face, the hollow eyes, the pelt of week-old bristles on his gaunt cheeks: he had the look of a winter-starved lobo overhungry for a kill. The old-timer he'd cast his glare on felt worse than from a winter's chill. He'd wet his pants from fear.

Now the big man stalked the street, mouth dry, hankering for a drink.

However, his quest was about to be curtailed by a scuttling lawman. Sheriff Harley Quade came down the jailhouse steps with stumpy legs pumping. He intercepted Cutter just outside the Ophir Gem, a small saloon with a sign eight feet long and as gaudy as a circus banner. The pair spoke above tinkling piano chords played by unskilled hands.

The lawman was angry and said so. "I'm plumb mad!"

He talked to Cutter's impassive profile. "That so?" the big man said, casually rolling a quirly.

"Them fellas tossed outa that upstairs window of the Sunflower! The clerk's declared the room they

92

come outa was yours! What's the big idea?"

Cutter exhaled Dixie Queen gray smoke. "Some you win, some you lose, I reckon. Those two weren't smart, and so they lost."

"They got hurt bad in the falls they took. Folks as was watchin' seen 'em walk off all stove up."

Cutter looked straight past Quade. "I ain't no doctor, Sheriff." He spotted the Longhorn Saloon displaying a boldly lettered card announcing a free lunch.

"I don't cotton to fracases, mister," Quade maintained. "Nor do I like them as cause 'em often. Last night three men died in this street. Today two more fellas got hurt. You were at the other end of a gun from all five. Plus I got suspicions about another one, our town newspaperman, 'Tribune' Tomlinson."

"Puts out readable sheet, from what I hear."

"Declares he cut hisself accidental-like. But witnesses state you were in the room when it happened."

Cutter's shrug had had a lot of practice since he'd come to Bitter Wash. "Wasn't watching the owner every minute. Was catching up on reading the news." He filled his lungs with smoke, then blew some across Quade's bow. "It happen you hear about a ranch family wiped out, Sheriff? Real massacre."

The lawman swabbed his red face with a green bandanna. "I knew all three Vandermeers. Them boys was ornery cusses, picky 'bout the water rights they claimed for their spread. Some firewater-ornery braves rode through, and the brothers and sister Emily got theirselves picked up and put in coffins. Undertaker Snee, he said—Hey! What's that t'do

93

with Tomlinson's sliced ear?"

"Nothing. Can't fool you, Sheriff. You're too smart. Now, if you'll excuse me, I was heading to a saloon."

"I'm tellin' you, mister, you ain't welcome in this town!"

Cutter's hand streaked toward his hip. Quade flinched. Cutter's hand clawed and scratched his leg. "Could've come up against bedbugs in that hotel room where I stayed. Seems more than one kind of pests need squashing hereabouts."

He turned his back on the flustered lawman and marched off up the street. He passed by the rowdily noisy Longhorn, and turning into a set of brightly painted batwings farther along.

"So you dropped by after all," Hollis Jowett said, just inside the roomy barroom of the Silver Horseshoe.

Cutter squinted past the gambler in the dimmer-than-outdoors light. He beheld a redwood bar thirty feet long, lined with drinkers from end to end. A wide mirror backed a bottle-ranked rear bar, and an enormous painting of a bosomy nude topped that. Coal-oil lamps hung on chandeliers made from wagon wheels, the whole works suspended from ceiling beams.

Cutter hoped the beams were strong, although they had held thus far. There was an air of splendor in the establishment, despite odors from spilled beer, uncorked whiskey and the cheap perfume of the whores.

Tables stood along the back and side walls of the place, and Cutter made his way toward one.

Poker chips clacked, playing cards swished, and a

roulette wheel hummed in the rear given over to gambling. Occasionally a participant in a game vented a curse, but it was a quiet crowd of patrons, with which any saloonkeeper should have few complaints. Jowett followed Cutter until he pulled out a chair and eased his bulk. A signal from the bearded gambler brought a glitter gal scurrying. Her low-cut dress showed a lot of breast and ended at her knees. Her rouged face had seen better days.

"Name your pleasure, friend. Mona, here, will fetch it pronto."

"Whiskey," Cutter declared.

"Make it a glass of my private stock, Mona. Mind if I join you, Cutter? I'm assuming that you've changed your mind and came on business."

"You assume wrong."

A questioning stare.

"Why am I at your place, Jowett, over the ones Wendell runs? I want a drink, not a goddamn fight. A matter of preference today only."

"Maybe you should reconsider. Things have changed some since this morning."

Cutter dragged on his smoke until the coal glowed, then dropped it and crushed it out.

"See those *hombres* at the bar?" Jowett pointed. "New men that just rode in to back my play. I sent word to Cheyenne, Deadwood, Dodge, and the high pay I offered brought 'em here. I'm getting ready to move, Cutter, and you can still take part. You can't hope to take on Bert Wendell alone. Look what happened to the Vandermeers."

Past Jowett's shoulder Cutter sized up the bunch of gunslicks the saloonkeeper indicated. No fewer than five huddled around a bottle on the bar, all

95

drinking steadily, but far from drunk. They wore the tied-down holsters and cared-for weapons of experienced guns for hire, and gazed about with malicious scowls.

"You know what really happened out at the Spade 8?"

Jowett smothered a cough. "I made it a point to call on undertaker Snee. Saw the boys and the gal laid on the zinc-topped table. Shot, but not scalped." The gambler thrust his face near Cutter's. "The fact of the cover-up shows Bert Wendell's power in this town. The undertaker's quaking in his boots. So's that newspaperman. Nobody in the street's mentioning the battle over water rights, the Spade 8's sweet spring, or the neighboring Wendell spread's thirsty stock."

A nod from the big man. The glitter gal set down a glass in front of him, and the amber liquid caught lamplight and gleamed. Mona shot a look at Cutter, her carmined mouth turned down. She pressed the tray to her front and turned away.

Cutter picked up the glass and tossed down the whiskey. The good-quality rye kindled a warm fire in his belly, but didn't lull him.

"I said that nobody in Bitter Wash stands up to Wendell," Jowett rushed on, wheezing. "The bastard wants to get his hands on this saloon, my share of the town's drinking and gambling take, plus the whores. But I'm a tough nut, Cutter, and one day soon my men and his'll meet head-on. He'll go down, and I'll come off winner, by God! And this town will rest easy at last."

Cutter set the glass down. "Maybe. How come you ain't beat him before now?"

Hollis Jowett frowned. He stroked the brownish goatee and licked his lips. "You're guessing that I've tried more than once, and that's correct. Set up ambushes that failed and skirmishes between my men and his men. Indecisive. Somehow Wendell was on the alert every time. That's not surprising, I suppose, considering the network of folks beholden to him. Still—?" He paused. "But now I've brought in those gunsels at the bar and more, besides. I'm countin' on the pattern gettin' changed."

"I ain't a part of any play of yours, Jowett," Cutter snapped. "Always work on my own. Got no need for that big pay you always talk on." He pulled out a banknote and held it between his fingers. "That's why I'm paying for the drink I had here. Plus what I aim to do next. That gal Mona—"

Jowett hacked a cough and used his handkerchief. It came away from his lips pink-flecked. "Yeah, the gal's for customers' use. Just tell her what you want, then ante up with the bartender. Her crib, all the cribs, they're right up those stairs."

"Obliged, Jowett."

Cutter turned from the saloon owner and moved through the crowd of drinkers toward the rear of the large room. Most of those men who saw him coming melted from his path. Those who didn't he shouldered past roughly, but nobody complained. He spotted a woman in red a good deal younger than Mona was. He bypassed her and a prettily smiling blond, as well.

When he reached the bar he asked "How much?" of the bar dog.

"Ten."

Cutter laid down greenbacks and moseyed past

baize-topped tables and the players at them. A dour faro dealer pumped a card from the wooden dealing shoe, and Cutter heard a player groan. The dealer raked in the bet and looked up questioning. "Oh, hell, yeah, I'll bet again." The fleeced gent dug deeply in his trouser pocket.

"I guess you want to go upstairs with me?" Mona, at the foot of the stairs, rubbed herself enticingly against Cutter. She smelled of rice powder, rose perfume and perspiration. Her breasts were soft as feather pillows.

"Upstairs, downstairs. Just so's it's the lady's chamber."

"Come on, mister. Follow me."

They climbed arm-in-arm and side-by-side, and on reaching the second story proceeded along a narrow hall. From behind curtained doorways could be heard assorted grunts and bedframe squeaks. Stopping in front of a quiet portal, the glitter gal gestured. "In here."

"Not much privacy."

"Enough." She pulled the curtain shut behind them, and before Cutter could say more, she'd popped open the top of her dress. Although the breasts were as large as the costume had promised, they were sagging, pendulous. The puckered nipples she'd painted with rouge.

She was undoing the fastenings of the flouncy skirt when Cutter hissed at her. "Far enough, Mona, if that's your real name."

"It's my name, all right. What you got in mind, mister? Whatever it is, your banknote's bought it."

"How many greenbacks has Bert Wendell paid you?"

The face sagged suddenly and the last of the woman's attractiveness was lost. "Huh?"

His hand shot out and took her by the throat. "We're going to palaver, Mona, soft-like, so's not to bother the folks next door. It ain't pleasant, being disturbed in bed."

"I'll tell you nothing, you son of a bitch!"

Cutter's open hand swung and caught her, slamming the dyed head against the bedpost. "Let's just see, whore. Let's just see!" He shoved her down on the straw-leaking pallet. From his sheath he drew his Bowie, first clapping his palm across her mouth.

The eyes bulged, and tears of fright smeared her cheeks.

"You want to change your mind, that's a female's right, I hear. Meantime—" Cutter dug with his knife point under Mona's round chin. Although not as tender as a truly young girl's, the skin cut easily and bled. Drops of crimson splashed the breasts—and Cutter's hand and the bed.

His voice growled insistently. "You're on Wendell's payroll; you're the spy in Hollis Jowett's nest. I saw the look in your eyes when the gambler was jawing down there. Your ears pricked like a spooked filly's at talk of his war with kingpin." His teeth showed between his lips. He might have been a panther feasting on its prey.

In actuality, he was a revenge-bent demon.

"So, gal, you going to own up?"

Behind his clasped fingers, a nod.

"No yells, no quick moves?"

A rapid, hard shake.

"I'm taking my hand off your mouth, so's you can

confess, give an angle to get inside Wendell's mansion—"

But as soon as she was loose, Mona spun away from the big man. She reached for the china basin on the washstand and snatched it up. She tried to deliver it with a roundhouse swing at Cutter, but failed. He caught her wrist in mid-arc.

She tried to yelp.

The fist he clenched around the knife rammed to her chin, and there was a crisp *crack* sound. Mona sagged, but her broken face sagged more, as she slipped to the floor. Blood drooled onto the filthy floor from gums cut by bashed teeth.

"Shit," Cutter breathed.

"Hey, everything all right in there?" The whore in the next crib owned a voice shrill as a bugle.

"Just fine!"

"Figured as much!"

Mona was unconscious. Her breathing rasped irregularly past bloody lips. She was bound to stay out for a good long time. The big man sheathed his weapon, smoothed his lank hair and straightened the Stetson, then stepped into the hall. Another of the soiled doves was making her way along it, holding up a bleary-eyed, sheets-in-the-wind cowpuncher. This woman had raven hair and her skin was as smooth as warm honey.

"Have a good romp with Mona, did you mister? Try me next time. I like big and fierce-lookin' gents. Ask for Carlotta, and I'll drop whatever I'm doin'."

In order to cut conversation short: "Maybe I just will, sister."

There was a back flight of rickety stairs, and

100

Cutter used them. Outside he found dusk descending on the town. He wiped Mona's blood from his hands onto his pants, then hitched his gunbelt to ride more comfortably.

He set a course and strode toward Myrt's café.

Chapter 12

Myrt cowered in a dank, chilly corner of the underground chamber where wisps of spiderweb strung through air redolent of mold and rats. Moisture sheened the granite-block walls, visible in the beams of a dim lantern. A steady-drip-drip of water was the only sound she could hear beside her heart.

She was petrified with fear.

The hands lashed behind her were pressed to rough, cold stone. There was still feeling in them, but not much, so tight were the knots at her wrists. The swollen fingers felt the size and shape of sausages. Myrt's back ached, and so did her tousle-haired head.

They'd clubbed that head hard, the men who'd brought her here after the terror in the café's kitchen. She'd looked up from scrubbing pots after midday mealtime, and they were rushing in to grab her. With no onlookers the pair had no trouble dragging her out back. Tied hand and foot, she'd revived to find herself in this foul place. Hours had passed. By now leg cramps made her think she'd never stand again.

A rat on the floor paused and sized up the bound human being boldly. Myrt cringed. The disgusting creature went into a hole.

Now the footfalls that had scared the rat registered on the woman's ears, and tears flowed freely. At the far end of the long cellar a door opened to show the legs of men descending stairs. When they reached bottom, the three strolled leisurely toward the captive until they stood over her. She had the impression of very shiny boots, and then she raised her eyes.

She gasped frantically and began to struggle.

One of the men — the brawniest and meanest-appearing — carried a leather-thonged riding quirt. But there were no horses down here to discipline, and so . . .

"Stop your squirming, woman! Did she give you trouble on the way here, Frank?"

"Boss, no trouble at all."

The one she recognized as an abductor, the second she'd seen in the café on a few occasions. The third was older, bald, and wore a mustache that curved like a downturned horseshoe around a tight, cruel mouth. Bert Wendell.

"Reckon she'll spill what she knows?"

"I'm confident she'll tell everything."

Frank Gideon stepped close. "Shall we string her up by the thumbs? Strip her? Whip her where she lays?"

Myrt's heart thumped at triphammer speed.

"Maybe none of what you mention will be necessary." Wendell peered down his haughty beaklike nose at the woman. Her rumpled dress was hiked high around her thighs. The hair was a fright. The jowled face was a mask of worry, and understandably so. She was at the end of her tether, and the next few minutes might leave her scarred, or blind, or worse. The bald man relished having her in this position. He felt his pants tight over bulging privates.

"W-what do you want from me?" she managed to stammer.

"All right, I'll tell you." Bert Wendell said softly. "You, Myrt, are well known in Bitter Wash. Bad morals took you low, and then a man named Chester gave you a job. Chester was, er—a local restaurant owner."

Myrt gulped and waited. Frank Gideon tapped his whip on his boot.

"Now Chester is dead. Killed twenty-four hours ago, almost. In the street with three others, who happened to be my cousins once removed on my mother's side of the family."

Snakes stared at their prey the way Wendell stared at Myrt. She was trembling now from toes to scalp. Her bladder leaked, and she felt her petticoat grow wet.

"Chester," continued Wendell, "went to Max Donovan in a saloon, warned that a dangerous stranger was out to get him. When Donovan went outside, he was confronted. When the smoke cleared, only one man walked away from the fight: the stranger. Nobody will say where he is now. But I want you to tell me, Myrt."

With tears streaking her blubbering face, she attempted a smile. "Sure, Mr. Wendell. S-sure.

You don't got to whip. I don't like the big bastard with the mean look, not no more than you. Th- the trouble i-is, I don't know much—"

The quirt slapped Gideon's boot loudly.

"Don't hit me!" squealed the woman. "See, the big man came to the café, asked after Donovan, but neither me or Chester'd tell. Then he beat up Chester, swore he'd kill us. Then Chester took him over to the Palace. What happened next, Chester caught some slugs. Now I'm alone as I ever was in the world. But I got to tell about the stranger! He went in the hotel that night. And I seen him in the street this morning, watchin' the hearse come down the hill. And he carries a Colt in a holster, and a hideout gun. Rides him a bay bronc."

"Ha!"

Bert Wendell scrubbed his baldness with a palm, and gnawed a mustache end. His slat-thin form inside his shirt quivered as if with chill. His restless eyes stilled and his face relaxed. "I believe you," he went on to Myrt. "I think you've told all you know. The scared-rabbit look on your face convinces me."

She sighed and slumped in her bonds, relieved. "Then you'll turn me loose?"

"You don't know us here too well." He turned to Frank Gideon. "I see no reason why the slut's cooperation should deprive you men of pleasure. Toss her outside when you've done all you want," Wendell directed. "Let her walk home. And yes, she can have her clothes, the rags." The nattily attired man turned on his heel and stalked away.

Myrt groaned as the light of the lamp went out for her. Then the hurting started, and went on for a long time.

Chapter 13

Cutter peered through the darkened window of the shabby café on Main Street, saw no one and nothing beyond the grimy glass. Then he began pounding on the door. After a full minute and with a scraped-raw knuckle, he quit in order to consider the situation. He didn't know where the proprietress was. And he knew it unfair to blame her for clearing out. Still, the hair at his nape prickled with a strong hunch, the same notion that had brought him down here so late.

"I believe Myrt's closed for the night and gone off someplace."

The big man spun, his hand streaking for his Colt. Then he saw who'd spoken from the shadows under the porch roof, and his big, muscular frame slumped in relaxation.

"What makes you think so?" he queried Cyril Wilkes.

The Easterner answered with a brittle New England twang. "I made a deduction is all. She was cooking food and serving it earlier in the day, but now she's not. We customers who've come out for a good dinner are just going to have to make do."

The young man cocked the head in the funny

dude's hat and slapped his jodhpur-clad leg. "I believe I saw you this morning outside the newspaper office." He thrust out a hand to be shaken. "How d'you do? Cyril Wilkes is my name. New in the West, but trying to meet all the residents out here I can."

"To each his own, I reckon." Cutter didn't take the man's hand.

In the glow of the streetlight Wilkes retained his grief-stricken look, red about the eyes, his mouth drawn down in harsh creases. "I hope you'll excuse my appearance and choked-up voice," he said. "It's been a bad day for me, I'm afraid. Damned sorrowful."

"You found out your lady-friend's dead, the one you aimed to tie the wedding knot with."

A sniff, a wipe of the face with a muslin sleeve. "Why, that's absolutely right. Can I take it you're another friend of the Vandermeers?"

"I ain't friends to many folks. But it happens I did meet the gal Emily once."

Cyril Wilkes sighed. "Emily! Portrait of virtue! Model of womanhood! Our married life would have been such bliss!" Then the young man's voice broke: "But now that hope's lost for ever. The girl is dead, killed by—"

"Redskins?" Cutter neglected to quell a snort.

Wilkes became alert. "Do I catch doubt in your tone, mister?"

Cutter started to turn away.

"Wait!" Wilkes's gaze was sharply focused. "I saw you leave the *Tribune* premises, and there was something strange about you then. You must've read the account of the raid. You must've suspected chicanery, as I do!"

108

"Look, mister, I come to get something to eat."

"Then I'll feed you, and we can talk about this whole matter! I rent a cottage just nearby at the town's edge, and I've supplies laid by. Nothing fancy, but we'll fare suitably, I assure you. I've been practicing my own kind of cookery."

"How far is this place of yours?"

Five minutes later Cyril Wilkes's leased walls surrounded the pair. He lit a coal-oil lantern on a deal table, then stood back to gesture. "I took this place on first arriving in Texas to work at my art. I guess you know I create landscape paintings, Mr., er—?"

"Just between you and me, Wilkes, the name's Cutter."

"The West's a wonderful place for a painter, Mr. Cutter, an inspirational place. In my months spent in Bitter Wash, my work's burgeoned in quantity and quality. Of course, a good part of that was Emily's influence." He slammed a hand down on the table. "Damn! Mr. Cutter, won't you help find her real killers? You seem a capable man! The law in this town's no use!"

"You've complained to the sheriff?"

"Quade? He's an ass!"

"That's two of us have it figured out."

The artist's nod was curt. "I'll just light the fire, prepare a meal, and relate everything I know and suspect. There was a mortgage on the Vandermeers' spread, for one thing. And the brothers were expecting trouble, but didn't take me into their confidence. Neither did Emily. Then she mysteriously insisted on riding off on her own yesterday." He clapped a pan down on an ancient Bailey stove. "I intend to get to the bottom of it! Stay in the house with me here tonight, and we'll make plans!"

"Whoa! First the food, and then the palaver."

"I have game hen, from the local market hunter."

"Whatever's handiest."

While the young man busied himself, Cutter peered about the old, ramshackle cabin. Besides the stove there were only a few furnishings: a deal table, two spindle chairs, a battered bunk with a pallet and a couple of quilts. Most of the room was given over to artist's supplies and gear. Stretched canvases leaned against all four walls, some unused but most of them finished paintings of local scenes.

On an easel stood a sketch of a rider aboard a bucking roan. It had been years since Cutter had last topped broncs, but he recognized Wilkes's mistakes easily. The horse's legs were wrong, likewise the painted puncher's position. The only thing correct about the scene was the sky of summery blue.

"I call that work 'The Bronco,'" Wilkes said over the rattle of pans. "The model is the Vandermeers' ranch hand Escobar. The Mexican hasn't been seen since—"

Cutter finished for him. "Since before the raid."

Wilkes went on cooking, his face locked in a frown.

An hour later both men pushed aside emptied plates, and leaned back in their chairs. "There's

110

more hot coffee," Wilkes stated.

"I'd be obliged."

As he poured cupfuls from the pot, the artist wound up his tale. "That about tells it, Mr. Cutter. What I have to go on is mainly hunch. I had inklings on visits to the Spade 8 that Joe's and Dave's enemy was a dangerous sort."

Cutter scratched a lucifer, touched flame to the quirly between his lips. "Yeah, I see." With his free hand he scratched the stubble he'd still not bothered to shave. "Well, Wilkes, I reckon I'll be on my way. I'll pay for the grub you served up, worth more than café fare any day—"

Wilkes jumped up and drew up to his five-and-a-half-foot height. "I didn't ask you here to be your servant, Cutter! I don't need your money! My father owns factories in Connecticut! Our family's quite wealthy, in fact!" Then some calm returned to his tone. "Let me tell you what I've decided. I'll buy the Spade 8 from the bank, paying off the Vandermeers' loan. I've learned to love these Texas hills and plains, and the ranch Emily called home will always have meaning to me! Tomorrow before the burials, I'll go to the bank and negotiate with Murdock! Arrange for legal transfer of deed—"

"Don't move!" Cutter's face became granite, the anthracite eyes glittering lustrous ice. The big man's hand leaped to his Colt as he spoke, and now he jerked the weapon, brought the barrel level and steady.

"What—" Wilkes blurted, pale as chalk.

"When I say freeze, do it!" The .44 bore aimed point-blank at the artist's throat. Then it twitched to the left a hair, and the big man eared the sliphammer with a thumb. Cyril Wilkes trembled in his boots, ready to fall on his knees, but Cutter's words held him erect. The innocent eyes were wide as saucers and stared into space.

Cutter's finger tightened on the trigger. The gun went off with a roar.

"My God!" Cyril Wilkes spun away from the blast, hand at the cheek that sustained the muzzle-flash burn.

The headless viper from the windowsill behind the artist thrashed harmlessly on the floor. "Copperhead," Cutter said. "Give no warning like rattlesnakes do, but they're poison as sin."

"How can I thank you, Mr. Cutter?"

"Let me stretch out by your fire tonight."

"Y-yes, of course. But why — ?"

"Let's say the hotel don't suit. Snakes and all, this shack's a heap safer."

Chapter 14

Dawn was a pewter-and-pink blaze above the hills to the east as Hector Escobar staggered to his feet groggily. Somewhere up the gulch a wren chattered, and close by a wary fieldmouse peered from under low mesquite. The man groped on the ground, clutched an empty mescal bottle, then hurled it aside in disgust. The shattering glass startled the horse hobbled in long grass beside the spring. The dun snorted, but didn't bolt.

With swarthy features showing all his forty years and then some, Escobar walked to the mount, stroked the sleek neck and heard the welcoming nicker. The fine animal wore the Spade 8 brand on its rump, had been broken by the Mexican hand for his employers.

Sometimes when he drank strong spirits while on the range the Mexican felt guilty. This time he did not. He'd bought the mescal, not pilfered it. Dave and Joe Vandermeer need never know his offense: this spring of fresh, cold water was a full two-day ride from ranch headquarters. Escobar merely stretched that to three, and he'd use the excuse that he'd needed to dig silt out of the stream channel.

Escobar's only trouble, really, was the headache, the dull alcohol haze that plagued him this morning after he'd gotten so drunk. He cupped a handful of water to his thick lips—and swore. "*Madre de Dios.*" The reaction of his stomach persuaded him to skip breakfast, launch immediately into the hazing of strayed cattle out of the brush and onto the flat.

After that chore he would head back and sleep that night in a snug bunkhouse.

Right now, however, he heard the fast approach of racing hooves, a series of harsh yells just beyond the rock shoulder above the spring. Then into view burst fleeing cattle led by a mossy-horned steer, wild-eyed and crazed. The knot of cows charged down the draw toward the Mexican, who scrambled from their path. Next the riders rounded the bend, hazing hard. The men were strangers, and the beef they stampeded carried the Spade 8 brand.

Rustlers.

Escobar put his hand to his old Starr Army Model, left the sixgun holstered, but stepped from concealment into the riders' path.

"*Hola, hombres!* Hey, what you doing with Vandermeer cows? This all Spade 8 ranch land! So *vamos!*"

They were five lasso-swinging, swearing horsemen, who pulled their mounts into haunch-down, sliding halts. Dust billowed about the jaspers, but failed to conceal their infuriated looks. The way their hands flew to weapons revealed practiced hardcase ways. In an instant Escobar faced cocked

114

Winchesters and Colts, five unwinking dark bores trained on him.

The Mexican gulped.

"Vandermeers' land? Haw!" The leader's bushed brows beetled. His mouth locked in a sneer. "No, boys, don't shoot the Mex down. That'd be too easy for him. Oliver, toss a loop, take him off'n his feet!"

Hector Escobar felt the snaking rope encircle arms and chest, felt himself jerked as the nooseman's horse tightened a dally around the saddlehorn. At the same time the wind was punched from his lungs and he toppled heavily. Flinty stones of the ground dug his backside. Mocking laughter filled his ears.

"What you got in mind, Weems?" a hardcase asked.

"How 'bout a goddamn test? Test the lariat, for openers. Throw the rope over that branch and hoist the Mex."

A minute later Escobar, arms pinioned, was suspended by the rope that circled his chest. His feet danced in air inches above the ground. He could scarcely breathe. Pain seared where the rope's tightness dug him. "All right, fellas! Target practice! Just make sure no bullets kill him right off!"

A rapid spattering of gunfire echoed in the draw, shots thrown carelessly or carefully by the lined-up tormentors of the Spade 8 cowhand. Most of the slugs ripped Escobar's clothes on his arms, sides, legs, laying fire-fierce graze marks into the skin to make blood ooze and elicit barks of pain from the man. Some hot lead splatted the boulder face near his head, shearing granite chips the size of dimes, and hurling them. The razor-sharp splinters chewed the Mexican's nose, cheeks and lips, mangling and slashing. His shining hair was dyed crimson, and the same color smeared his features.

The torture did not let up, even when guns were emptied. The man called Weems urged his gelding close, grasping his Winchester by the barrel and swinging the long gun. The hard brass breech slammed Escobar's temple, laying it open in a jagged cut, extremely hurtful.

Escobar's shriek of agony rent the heavens and the man's whole body quaked at the end of the rope. Magpies in nearby trees sprang into flight. Jackrabbits shrank into the juniper brush, cowering.

Then all other sounds were drowned by hard-case laughter as the five whooped obscenely, pointed and slapped their knees. "Haw, look at 'im!"

"Damned Spade 8 rider Mex!"

"Serves him right, punchin' cows for th' Vandermeers!"

Weems shouted above the rest. "Cut the goddamn rope! Drop him!" When the Mexican was sent rolling and twitching on the ground, the ramrod commented sarcastically, "Y'know, I ain't too scared the Mex'll make it home, tell his bosses all 'bout us Rockin' W fellas!"

"Hell, Weems," Oliver slurred, "them squatter Vandermeers, they're already—"

"Shut up!" The ramrod threw a broad wink at

116

his sidekicks. "I said the Mex just might reach ranch headquarters and get a sawbone's help. But, since we're takin' his bronc, he'll need to go afoot!"

"Won't that still be too easy for 'im?"

"You may be c'rect!" He called another man to his side. "Hey, Scott!"

"Yeah," the ugliest member of the bunch rasped. The man had hair that was gray as a sick rat's fur, and blemished skin of almost the same color. He dismounted at the leader's signal, his shelving forehead pinched into a frown.

"What d'you suggest, if we want the Mex t' travel slow? Bust his feet up, maybe?"

"Good idee, Weems. I'll take care of it."

The man called Scott worked Escobar's boots off, and then proceeded to use his carbine's hardwood stock to hammer unmercifully at the victim's bare feet. Sweat rolled down his face with his effort. With each mutilating, thudding blow, Escobar coughed like a leash-whipped dog. After a while the punished parts turned purplish, here and there splintered bones piercing the skin to show pearl-white. Finally finished with the victim, the rifle-wielder put up his piece, marched to his horse and hauled into the saddle.

"*Adios, amigo!*" Weems called, echoed by his pards. "If you get to Bitter Wash, stop by the Palace!" He clapped spurs to his mount, and the outfit galloped off.

Hector Escobar writhed on the ground, bearing his agony as best he could. His harsh sobs eventually turned to groans.

117

He knew he'd never crawl the twenty miles he needed to go. He'd die in this place, he thought. Die and end up buzzard meat.

Still, with an effort of will he managed to look around with pain-reflecting eyes, heave onto scraped elbows.

He pointed himself south and crawled.

The preacher in the black suit swept off his hat and opened the large book that he clutched in soft hands. "Folks, we're called together on a sad occasion," he intoned in a mellifluous voice. "David, Joseph and Emily Vandermeer will today be laid to their eternal rest—"

To the rear of the crowding men and women who flocked the graveyard, Cutter watched coldly, hand fidgeting in his pocket. He absently fingered the coiled piece of wire he carried ever-handy: his death-dealing garrote. The religious rite held no importance for him, although he approved of getting rid of rotten bodies.

His eyes fixed on Cyril Wilkes in the forefront of the mourners, the sleeve of his broadcloth suit swathed in funeral crepe. Already that morning, before the appointed hour for the funeral, the artist had stopped by the bank, tendered a cash offer for purchase of the Spade 8 ranch. The deal was being considered by cashier Murdock. All this because of Wilkes's feeling for dead Emily's memory.

The big man shook his head. And yet his own view affirmed each man's right to go to hell however he chose. That his own had become a killer's path he accepted totally. As nobody could dissuade him from the tasks he'd set, he'd refrain from correcting Wilkes.

If the artist's bumbling brought the evil forces of Bert Wendell down on him so be it.

And if the land-grabber was pulled into Cutter's net as a result, the big man wouldn't complain. He'd kill the bastard.

Gazing up the street toward the foot of Mansion Hill, the big man saw a shiny new buggy roll onto the flat. The polished paint of the rig gleamed and the matched mares stepped smartly in the traces. The folded oilcloth top let morning sun fall on the passenger. This well-dressed gent — slat-thin, hatchet-featured — wore a prodigious mustache and puffed a pipe. This was Bert Wendell, just as Cutter had pictured him.

There wasn't much difference between the branding-iron-wielding bastard of thirteen years ago and now. He was just as mean and vicious-looking today as he had been then.

The difficulty was, the man wasn't much of a target. He was more than three hundred yards off, and Cutter had no rifle along. Also, between the big man and Wendell rode six guards who surrounded the buggy — in front, in the rear and to both sides.

Still, Cutter didn't aim to let a chance pass. He turned from the preacher's solemn droning and broke into a long-strided lope toward the buildings in the center of town. He dodged among standing wagons and their teams, tied saddle horses and

119

people on the boardwalk who were not attending the funeral. As the buggy carrying Wendell approached, Cutter reached to draw his sixgun.

His eyes lifted to the roofs across the street. Atop the Silver Horseshoe Saloon, above the tall false front, Cutter spotted a man. He recognized one of Hollis Jowett's gunslingers from yesterday. The gunsel clutched a Winchester.

Wendell's rig rolled to a stop outside the bank. The gunsel poised and took careful aim at Wendell's narrow back. Wendell leaned forward to strike a match and light his pipe.

The rifle slug whizzed past Wendell's neck, sheared a foot-long sliver from the rig's seat. At the gun's bark, Wendell spun sharply, then hit the floorboards as the team bolted and the rig took off. Instantly the bodyguard of six had their guns out and fired a withering fusillade at the lone shooter.

The man on the roof took a bullet in the chest and flung his rifle away. Then, lined in relief against the brilliant sky, he caught more slugs all over his stocky frame. Each of these made impact with shuddering force, and the silhouetted form jerked absurdly on the saloon roof, then lurched from the edge and plunged toward the porch roof. The hurt jasper struck it with a crunch, bounced, then rolled. From there he toppled again, this time landing across a sturdy hitchrail.

A woman standing nearby screamed.

The victim hung grotesque and unmoving, his back broken.

Cutter powered into motion, Colt at the ready,

legs a pumping, sprinting blur.

Wendell's six riders yelled in unison and spurred their mounts in the direction of the big man. The buggy followed behind its galloping team, Wendell crouched behind the splashboard.

Guns opened up, and a blizzard of lead erupted.

Chapter 15

Cutter dropped behind a spooked, sunfishing buckskin at a hitchrail, as other wild-eyed horses in the line tore at their tie-reins. One went down thrashing, shot through the neck, and the animal's kick devastated a trough to send water sheeting. Hot lead spattered both mud and boardwalk, spraying splinters that raked panic-stricken running folk. A crippled swamper's crutch snapped and he went sprawling. A soiled dove lost her ostrich-feather chapeau. An elderly crone pitched in soggy dung, rolled, and jumped up to flee, hysterical.

Cutter crawfished into a doorway and returned fire as Wendell's rig raced past. The shot missed, the cowardly kingpin diving behind the jehu. Gunsel riders formed a surging wall of horseflesh that couldn't be broached. Shrieks of passersby mingled with shots from shootists. Main Street was a model of hell.

Then the buggy tore around the corner and the pounding of hooves faded and was gone. A thick haze of dust hung in the street. All was eerily quiet.

Cutter glanced up and found himself on the

front stoop of the jail. Behind him the door opened; a drunk-sounding voice grunted: "God-damn son of a bitch!"

Sheriff Harley Quade showed himself. "You still round these here parts, mister?" he slurred. "Damn! I told you to clear out! Now you're hunkerin' on my doorstep. Big as life . . . hogleg in your f-fist." A sidelong look from the rheumy eyes. "*You* start that ruckus?"

It would have been funny if the tipsy badge-packer hadn't palmed a Smith & Wesson. It might have been hilarious if the sixgun weren't pointing at Cutter's gut.

"I never started the ruckus," the big man said levelly. "Maybe the gent in the rig did?"

The lawman's slack face scowled. "Th' gent, hell, that's Bert Wendell, mister. I do li'l jobs for him sometimes. Man just 'bout owns th' whole town. Why'd he want it shot up?"

"Beats me."

The big sixgun in the lawman's hand twitched. "Walk inside the jailhouse there, stranger. Pronto."

Cutter's gun was empty. The big man shrugged and obeyed the order.

"Quade, ain't you going to help the hurt folks? A shot-up fella fell off the saloon roof. There's horses need putting out of their misery. Lots to do, Sheriff. And you're fooling with me?"

"Into the cage, and no more jawin', by God! Drop the hogleg! Move!"

As soon as he entered the cell the barred door slid home on its track, clanging. It was the sound of jail doors the world around. Added to this occasion was the tipsy lawdog's laugh. "Mebbe I just will go out in th' street! Do good deeds! Swig from some dandy's flask!" Quade stepped to the door. "Mebbe there's gals who'll be plumb grateful to a rescuer!" A lewd chuckle broke from Quade. "Wait locked in where y'are stranger! Haw!"

He stumbled on the threshold, but succeeded in exiting, which left Cutter standing behind the bars alone. Nobody had emptied the last prisoner's piss out of the cell bucket, and it stank. The entire office was a mess of strewn wanted dodgers, bottles and general refuse.

Outside, voices lifted in complaints, and among them Cutter thought he caught Hollis Jowett's. There were hoofbeats and the rattle of wheels. Conveyances were again rolling in the street.

Cutter leaned hard against the rusty-barred cell door, and as he thought it might, it moved. Without more delay, the big man slid it open wide.

He stepped out and retrieved his Colt from the top of the littered desk, then holstered the weapon. He could reload later, elsewhere. But there was something that needed doing before he cleared out fast. He plucked up a pen and scrawled a note to Quade on a paper scrap, leaving the message unsigned.

The lone window opened onto an alley, which he let himself down to. He ran to the livery by way of a back route. He was up in the saddle of his bay in no time and set the gelding into a mile-eating lope, south.

* * *

124

"I tell you, Bert, there's no help for it," Giles Murdock said. The banker's eyes stared past Bert Wendell at a miniature statue in the corner of the mansion drawing room. Although of the same Italian marble as the mantel, the figure seemed possessed of a living glow. Perhaps it was the subject: an exquisite female nude. She was portrayed bending to pluck a hyacinth, and the banker imagined he could see the moon-round buttocks flex. "Ah . . . I seem to've lost my train of thought."

The gaunt-faced bossman of Bitter Wash twitched his bristly mustache, sat back in his stuffed wing chair, and scrubbed his chin with a palm. His features were more sharply chiseled this afternoon, the lines more deeply etched. Wendell remembered the ambush in the street and was aware of how close death had come. The thought gnawed his gut, though the event had occurred hours before.

His temper was on a short fuse.

"Damn you, Murdock! Spit it out, the reason you're here! Something about an offer to buy for the Vandermeer spread? Must be a damn lie!"

The banker shook his long-jowled head solemnly. "It's not only possible, it's happened. That Easterner Wilkes, he's puttin' his family money on the line. Cash offer, Bert, to pay off the dead Dutch folks' mortgage, and a bonus to boot. Can't refuse it without a reason."

Fingers drummed on the plush chair arm. "Cook up a reason!" Wendell paused. "No, wait!"

Near Wendell's corner of the drapery-hung room

dangled a damask pull cord, which the man now tugged. Silence reigned for a minute or two, and then Frank Gideon strode into the room. Standing on his bowed legs, hipshot, he listened to crisp orders drawled out. When Wendell was through giving them, Gideon stroked the hairs on his lip and grinned.

"Got it all straight?"

"Lemme see." Gideon half closed his eyes as he spoke, recapping. "You want me to send some o' the boys after the dude Wilkes. He's the fella as draws pictures o' the trees and such. You want him busted up, so's he'll decide to pack and move back East."

Wendell glanced at Murdock. "What'd I tell you, banker? The man's sharp and ruthless—like his boss." He wagged an index finger, pleased with himself. "No punches pulled, now, Gideon! The next stagecoach rolls through town on Friday. I want Wilkes on it!"

"Oh, he'll see the wisdom," the segundo assured. "That all for now, boss?"

"When Giles goes, we'll discuss the Jowett business."

"I'll be in the cellar. With the laundress who got behind in her rent."

Murdock found himself uncomfortable most times, dealing with Bert Wendell, but things were worse today than usual. Now mayhem—even bloodshed—seemed about to result. Still, he couldn't have neglected to reveal Wilkes's offer. Giles Murdock couldn't stand suffering, himself. And everyone who let Wendell down—failed to tender what was owed, tell what he knew—inevitably paid a price of suffering.

Murdock had a nice house in town to lose. What would his wife say if he lost it? What of his marriageable, schoolmarm daughter? Who'd protect the pretty thing? The banker didn't want the likes of Gideon badgering her. No, he wouldn't try to stand up against Wendell.

"You're dismissed, Giles."

"Huh?"

"Get out!"

Murdock got up, straightened his tailored clawhammer coat, but he knew he wouldn't depart in dignity. Where Wendell was concerned, no one ever did. The town boss always humiliated visitors. "Well, good day to you, then, Bert—"

Wendell turned his back and began stuffing his pipe with pungent tobacco.

On his way out, Murdock passed the sheriff, who entered with a stumble and clearing of throat. "Er, Mr. Wendell, sir—" The lawman stopped, eyes cast down at the rug. "Suthin' h-happened, and I reckon you oughtta know 'bout it—"

"What's it?"

"Well, it's l-like this," Quade whined. "I was able to grab the stranger that shot Donovan and the Dibbs cousins. The great big fella with the cold snake's eyes and the fast gun. Only, he got away again, almost as soon—" Quade shoved his pudgy paw to his mouth.

"Goddamn you!" Wendell was out of his seat and confronting the lard tub. "What? Let him get

127

away? You been drinking again?"

"Please don't sic Gideon on me! I'm here and tellin' you 'bout it all. And givin' you this!"

Wendell took the crumpled paper that Harley Quade held out. He read the words that had been scribbled by Cutter on leaving jail. The kingpin let his mood slide into rage. The predator's-beak nose flared, and the mouth opened in a howl: "Gideon!"

The segundo burst in, sixgun in his hand. "Gordy and Arlo are lookin' for the artist fella, boss. Just rode out a minute ago. Now what the hell—?"

"Get more men into the saddle and set to ride! I aim to do for the big son of a bitch, the one with the gun in his hand on Main Street this morning. He's huntin' me, sure as hell, with or without Jowett. He could even be behind killin' the guards we found today. Read this!"

The bossman's hand shook, but Gideon read: " 'You can tell Wendell I want him dead. He'll find me at the Spade 8—if he's not a yellow belly.' The stranger sent this note, boss?"

It was Sheriff Quade who bobbed his head. "I didn't mean t' leave th' cell door unlocked. Must not've—"

Wendell came around with the short, stiff riding whip he snatched from the mantel. He slashed the thong across Quade's face. The deeply split cheek and lips spurted a spray of blood droplets, some soiling Wendell's boiled shirt, most ending on the nude statue. The white surface was left speckled with red stains. The lawman staggered back, blub-

128

bering. "I-I didn't mean no harm!"

"Worthless idiot!" Then Wendell turned back to Gideon. "Get those riders ready, and have 'em armed to the teeth. Four ought to be able to handle the chore. Then get out to the Spade 8 to make coyote meat of the stranger."

"I savvy, boss."

"Tell the boys to kill the son of a bitch good! Carve him up first so's to teach Jowett a lesson!"

Chapter 16

A spruce and a dogwood shared the top of the round green hill with patched sage and a fisting outcrop of orange stone. Down the slope a swift, bubbling stream meandered. A high sun flooded the land with golden radiance.

Cyril Wilkes had wandered before to this restful site, but never to paint, his attention captured at those earlier times by far more striking views of canyonlands and ridges.

Today the artist felt drained, in need of the peacefulness in nature.

The death of Emily was the greatest tragedy he'd had to face in life. He'd loved his fiancée more deeply than he'd known. The tears he'd cried at her and her brothers' burials had far from eased his loss. Only serene, thoughtful periods would. The notion of buying the ranch she'd lived on had seemed a good one—yesterday. Then the banker had mouthed discouraging words, suggested he leave his new home in the West, and abandon his dream.

Now Wilkes was in this lonely spot to think. Here was cool shade and a pleasant, if not spectacular, vista. He'd felt moved to paint, recreate the scene. Now, his easel set on a strip of spike-grass, he'd made quick judgments on perspective, light and shade. He'd fished a sharpened charcoal stick from his paintbox, made some strokes on his canvas. He worked rapidly at his sketch, stopping only occasionally to squint and scan.

Then, during one of his pauses, he looked up and saw the far-off figure moving under the prairie sun. Wilkes shaded his eyes with a skinny hand. The object in the distance was approaching up the long slope with dreadful slowness. It seemed a man-sized slug, low to the ground, crawling.

Cyril Wilkes laid down charcoal and brush in the grass, rose from his stool and glanced at his picketed horse. No, he wouldn't take the mount, but investigate on foot. If it was a man, it was almost a dead one! Wilkes exerted his unconditioned, city-bred body, climbed over a rock ledge and angled, stumbling, down a terraced talus fan.

He reached the human remnant on a ledge above surrounding countryside that extended flat for miles. The fellow's garments were rags, frayed cloth strips that hung from battered arms, legs and torso. The apparition lurched toward the artist on hands and knees devoid of skin. He left a trail of blood. The man's feet were swollen like blown-up hog's bladders, double normal size. The ruptured skin oozed crimson from a hundred cuts.

Still Cyril Wilkes recognized him. "Escobar? Hector Escobar? My God!"

The slick boots of patent leather slipped on gravel, but the artist went on scrambling to reach the Mexican. When he succeeded, he knelt and tried to help the broken man. "Hector—"

Escobar's head swiveled on its stringy neck, showed a face that was sunburned horribly. Fire-red skin shredded from cheeks, forehead and chin. His bare shoulders were a mass of blistered sores.

There was insanity in the man's blank gaze.

Escobar, crazed from his ordeal, was invested with sudden madman's strength. He heaved up and grabbed the throat of his savior in a grip as tight as a vise. Wilkes cried out and fell back, afraid.

As the pathetic battlers rolled and wrestled, below on the flats a rider approached on a sleek, short-coupled bay. The man caught a flash of movement, and focused with the keen eyes of a hawk. Cutter's path would lead him past the fray, but he was unmoved by the fact. On his way to the Spade 8, he meant to make fast time. Two men wrestling on a hill needn't change his route, he calculated.

He gigged the bay onward at the same mile-devouring pace.

Hector Escobar, wild-eyed, slammed Cyril Wilkes's chest with a forearm. Rocketing pain engulfed the artist's ribcage, but he had the courage to battle back. His puny arms threw feeble punches, then wrapped his attacker and squeezed as hard as he could. A yowl from the crazy Mexican shrilled in Wilkes's ear. An elbow ground to his mouth and he tasted salty blood.

Meanwhile, Cutter, closer now, recognized one of the pair ahead tussling on the hillside. Cyril Wilkes. So the tenderfoot *did* have sand in his craw! Still, the big man remained stolid, emotionless, as he rode.

Wilkes was getting the worse of the fight. He

bucked violently under the weight of Escobar, each movement breaking more of the Mexican's blisters and popping slippery pus. The half-stripped man was difficult to grab. The dude's hands slid on the slimy flesh.

Powering a knee, he drove into the Mexican's groin. Escobar retreated like a scuttling scorpion, cursing in Spanish. But Wilkes heard another, simultaneous sound. He ceased rolling on the ground and looked up, saw a horseman rein his mount in to tower above him. He felt relief flood his mind.

"Cutter!"

"Howdy, Wilkes."

"I found this man crawling across the Spade 8 range. He's the Vandermeer brothers' cowhand, Hector Escobar—"

Escobar, at the sound of his name launched himself weakly at Wilkes's legs. Both fell to the ground, the Mexican kicking and gouging the artist. The shirt Wilkes wore was ripped, his riding pants were smeared with clay and blood.

Cutter nudged the bay toward the cutbank of the creek, his hand palming the canvas waterbag slung from his pommel. As the brawlers mixed it up, he stooped and filled the canteen with clear water.

"Cutter, for Christ's sake, help—!"

The big man corked the canteen tightly, then permitted the gelding to quench its thirst. Behind him he heard blows falling on yielding flesh, a series of harsh grunts. He cupped stream water in his hand and splashed his face to cool it.

"Cutter, I—"

The big man turned, peered with hooded eyes,

shrugged. "I got business at the Spade 8."

Now Cyril Wilkes, battered by the Mexican's fists, read Cutter's expression, and felt a chill. He saw his appeals didn't touch the indifferent big man at all.

He was on his own.

The bloody face of Escobar hung over Wilkes's own like a hideous moon. Mustering the last of his limited strength, the artist shoved knees to the Mexican's midsection and pushed, toppling him to at last stretch out still on the earth. Stentorian breaths rasped in the windpipe of knocked-out Escobar; he shivered once, then lay utterly still.

Cyril Wilkes rushed to him. "Jesus God!"

"No need to feel guilty," Cutter pointed out. "You didn't kill him, he did it to himself. The fella was loco from the pain." He shrugged.

"Men worse than animals are at large in this country."

"I don't doubt it." Cutter lifted the bay's reins.

"Hector once told me he had relatives in Willow Gulch. That's not far. I'll pack him to his family on my mare, tell what happened and express regrets."

Cutter lifted to the saddle. "Each to his liking." He gigged the bay.

Cyril Wilkes stood in the midst of nature's grandeur and viewed the ugly corpse at his feet. Cutter and his mount trotted into a stand of beeches and were gone.

The forlorn prairie wind sang.

Chapter 17

The four horsemen pushed their mounts hard across the broken country, the flats dotted with grazing longhorns left far back along the trail to Bitter Wash. The riders moved in a world of deep draws and steep outcrop slopes, spurring toward higher ground still, burnished gold by a westering sun. Between limestone ridges, stands of beech and cottonwood grew dense, requiring long detours. But they were getting close to the Spade 8 headquarters Squint Duran, the leader, knew.

The ugly man with the clouded white eye calculated an hour, perhaps less, to reach the fenced compound.

Although they'd left the town riding all abreast, now they strung out in ragged file. The punishing pace had taken its toll of men and horses both. But they were fighting time. Bert Wendell's time. The bossman had ordered death to the big, ornery stranger — today.

Duran turned in the saddle, the wind of passage flattening the brim of his hat against its crown. "Come on, boys! Don't slow now! We got our job cut out!" The party thundered over a ridge crest, then down into a swale. Duran was a gunsel who

135

enjoyed pleasing the boss, liked the rewards it brought in bonus money, liquor and whores.

But he also liked the work. Killing suited him and he was expert at it.

Now he led the band loping into the last draw before ranch headquarters. Ahead lay a towering vee of weathered granite that on the other side would open on the downslope. He reined up, and the others overtook and surrounded him, drawing in amid a cloud of dust. "We almost there?" the runtiest gunsel barked, doglike face puckering.

Duran answered crisply. "Bester, you're new in these parts, so I'll tell you somethin' one time. The corral, sheds and main house, they're all at the bottom of the hill. We'll file down gallopin' and shootin' Injun-style, to catch the bastard inside if we can. If that don't get him, we'll fire the place and roast him. The other boys, they know the lay of the land from shootin' up the Vandermeers t'other day. Now it's more of the same, fellas!"

He glanced from eager face to face, pleased with the anticipation of violence written in the expressions. These were hard-bitten gunslingers—Blackjack Holderman and Hank Moonlight—companions for years in Bert Wendell's employ. Young Lew Bester was a fresh import from down San Antonio way. Today would make a test for his skills.

"Boss Wendell didn't say it, but I'm sayin' it," Squint Duran rumbled in conclusion. "If the big stranger's hurt but not finished off, we get to play a mite with him. Teach him what pain feels like." A wicked leer. "Ain't sliced off a man's balls for a while."

136

All were grinning now except Moonlight, the gone-bad Choctaw tribesman — but then he always had a sour pokerface. Squint Duran readied himself to give the ride-out signal. But then his gaze strayed to the towering rock formation.

"Hey! Sunshine on metal! A goddamn ambush!"

Cutter peered down the barrel of his Winchester. He thumbed the hammer to full cock, put Duran in the sights. It had been a maxim of his teacher Ruiz: always take the enemy's leader out first. Finger squeezed trigger, the weapon boomed, and a slug hurtled.

An ounce and a quarter of pulverizing lead slammed the squint-eyed jasper's jaw, shattering it. White bone chips and red blood spattered the front of the sweaty shirt. The lower half of Duran's face collapsed to hang by tendon ends. The man catapulted from the saddle and bounced along the ground.

"Jesus! Up top! A rifleman!"

"Thought Squint said he'd be at th' spread!"

"Squint didn't know shit!"

The men yelled as they reined mounts about to flee, but Cutter had recocked swiftly and drawn a bead on the gent spurring away fastest and hardest. A bullet plowed his back and snapped his spine as he jerked like a puppet. He, too, dropped. Two men were dead, Duran and Lew Bester. Cutter jacked his rifle's action, aimed and tried to pick off Blackjack Holderman.

The gunsel's horse was running full-out downslope, and Cutter's shot missed. But Blackjack was firing back, snap shots over his shoulder with a sixgun. Hot lead zinged on the granite near Cutter, ricocheted, and the big man ducked.

But he reared up again and fired; this time the slug exploded the victim's head like a dropped pumpkin. Blackjack's hat kited away on a tide of mushed brain matter. Gore soaked the mount, saddle, the surrounding ground. The body of the man slammed down, then was trampled to jam by thudding hooves.

Deathly quiet filled the draw between the stone walls. Nothing could be seen moving. Cutter craned his neck and peered from concealment, but to no avail. He knew the fourth gunsel of the bunch was still alive, the Indian in white man's clothes. Then the big man glimpsed the tail of a horse switching flies behind a boulder.

The animal was a spotted pinto—the redskin's animal!

If the redskin had left his mount, he was scaling the heights to get the jump on the big man. Above and to his left, Cutter heard the rattle of a falling pebble.

He swung to see the tiny rock bound down the cliffside, then spun to face the other way.

Hank Moonlight launched himself, preceded by his knife. He was lightning on his feet, and the weapon he brandished had a wicked twelve-inch blade. But Cutter triggered the Winchester as Moonlight sprinted shouting in his infernal tongue. The Choctaw's kneecap exploded blood and bits of gristle, spilling him on the stony trail.

Cutter approached warily to see the glint of pain in Moonlight's agate eyes. Striking out like a cornered wildcat, the downed man darted with his blade, almost slashing Cutter's groin. The big man took a casual step to the side, stared down at the copper-skinned foe. There was no trace of anger to be seen in Cutter, merely cold contempt.

Without raising the Winchester, Cutter triggered from the hip. The report filled the defile with echoes, as the Indian was flung back, an extra hole punched in his forehead. There was no movement in the dead man, and the staring eyes immediately filmed over.

Cutter cast his gaze at the fast-declining day around him, then strode toward his waiting horse.

"What happened to Hector was a terrible tragedy, folks," Cyril Wilkes declared. "And I swear I'll do my best to make his torturers pay."

The old Mexican couple the artist faced stood in the center of their packed-earth farmyard, expressions frozen in the grief at the news of Hector Escobar's death. Trees surrounded the small clearing in the hills, and the floor of the swale was dotted with stumps from when farming had first been tried in the thin soil. The main structure was a log shanty from which a crooked stovepipe thrust. Stripped saplings formed an enclosure for pigs and goats — all sickly and emaciated.

Here and there chickens roamed and scratched the dirt. The couple had been preparing supper, and the smell of boiling fowl hung in the evening air. Wilkes rested against a chopping block littered with bloody plucked feathers.

"I brought the body across my mare's back while I hiked, leading her. I'll help to bury Hector, if you'd like."

Old Escobar swabbed his tears with a ragged

sleeve. "The burial, is nothing, *señor.* My wife Madelina and I, we are able. Old, but not too old for this."

"Well, if you folks are sure—"

The couple had built a fire to cook supper outdoors, and the flames under the stewpot gave light to the dusk-dark yard. Thus Wilkes spotted the sinister riders as they trotted their mounts up.

"Isn't it the practice out West to call 'Hello the yard,' or such?" Wilkes didn't like the looks of the pair, the pugnaciously jutting chins, the rifles drawn.

"Only if there's risk we'll get shot by some tough nut. Don't see none of those hereabouts." The menacing pards swung from the saddle to confront the Escobars and guest. They glanced at the horseblanket-wrapped bundle on the ground, saw it obviously was a corpse, and focused on Wilkes. "Mister, we been lookin' for ya!"

"That so?"

"Bet your ass!" The hardcase sneered. "Yeah, Arlo, here's the artist gent we seen in town more'n once. You rec'gnize him too?"

"Hard not to, Gordy." Arlo's face split in a black-toothed grin. "I mean, looka them sissy duds. Got his hair cut at the barber shop. Smell the Bay Rum stink-pretty?"

"I smell it, and I don't like it," Gordy snapped. "Fittin' for back East, you calc'late, dude?"

He'd sidled close to cow Wilkes, and, being a larger man, glared down balefully. The evening's shadows had advanced, and now the firelight was the major illumination. The Mexican couple tried to drift toward the shack, but were halted by a shout. "Hold it, greasers! Else your asses get

140

shot!"

Pedro and Madelina Escobar froze.

"Trying to scare all of us is a waste," Wilkes said. "If it's something to do with me, you can let the old couple go."

"Wilkes, you may just be right. Why make extra work when we got a plateful? Now, dude, we hear you like Bitter Wash?"

"I intend to settle here. Who told you two? The banker?"

"Somebody as thinks it'd be a mistake!" Arlo shoved the painter, sent him staggering into Gordy's grip. "The biggest mistake of your life!"

Gordy roughly spun Wilkes and pushed him back toward his pard. Wilkes stumbled into the chopping block, flinched when his hand touched a wrung-off chicken head. "Your threats don't scare—"

In the fire's flicker, Gordy's sixgun gleamed. It came up rapidly and pressed Wilkes's temple, steely and cold.

"We're told not to kill ya, artist fella. Just make you think hard 'bout stagecoachin' back East. We know you come out here to draw pictures, but if'n you can't, you got no purpose to squat. Ain't that fact?"

"There's my attachment to the beauty of the land—"

"Bullshit! Are you right- or left-handed, fella?"

"What d'you mean to do?"

As Gordy kept the gun on him, Arlo grabbed up an axe from the woodpile. It was a heavy, double-bitted implement. Behind him, Wilkes heard the Escobars gasp.

"*Madre de Dios!*"

141

"Shove the great artist over to the squared stump, Gordy!"

Cyril Wilkes's agitation had turned to fear. His stomach felt tight as a clenched fist, and was worsening by the second. The painter found himself bullied backward to the site of the chicken beheading, and his eyes picked out the brown stains on the ground, even by dim firelight.

"Did you hear him tell which he painted with— his right hand or his left?"

"Gordy, pard, I ain't heard a word."

"I'll hold down both his wrists on the stump, then. Ready with that tool?"

"I beg you, *señors*—" Pedro blurted.

The woman gasped incoherently.

Bob Gordy's frame was heavy with powerful muscle, and he made short work of wrestling the frail Easterner into position with his arms outstretched. Both Wilkes's forearms extended across the flat top of the block, the fingers on the pinned hands twitching spasmodically. Arlo powered the axe high, around and down in a vicious arc, and the razor edge crunched through skin, blood-vessels and bones, embedding solidly in the wood. Wilkes's severed hands flopped in the dirt like panfish, blood hosing from the stumps of wrists.

Wilkes's agonized shriek rang in the clearing, was repeated and went on. The penned animals cowered with their ears laid back, and frightened chickens sped into the woods.

Across the block from the amputated hands, Wilkes's body slumped and at the same time writhed. "Let's cut that bleedin'," Gordy grunted, dragging the victim to the blazing fire. Into the flames he thrust the gory wrist stumps, and

142

pumping blood was stanched in the cauterizing sear. Only then was Wilkes let fall like a cornhusk doll, still screaming.

"See any sense in lingerin', Arlo?"

"Can't say I do."

"Shit, let's ride for Bitter Wash." The men mounted and turned their horses toward town. When they were out of sight beyond the trees the Escobars approached the fire, shaken from shock.

"He is a good man," the Mexican woman murmured. "He returned our Hector's body to us."

"*Sí*, wife, we will tend him in his pain."

Cyril Wilkes ceased screaming abruptly, collapsed in a faint.

The rising moon shone palely on the squalid farm.

Chapter 18

"It's one of the best dinners I ever ate, Sarah Murdock!"

"Roast beef with sauce—I never saw juicier! And the cinnamon-nut bread! Plumb delicious!"

"You've outdone yourself!"

In the center of her banker husband's dining room, the hostess smoothed her dress of lavender dimity and beamed. She held her proud gray-streaked head high as she regarded her family and guests seated at table. Mr. and Mrs. Tomlinson, though not social equals, were a respectable enough couple in the Bitter Wash community. And it was important to count the newspaperman and wife as friends—at least, so her Giles had told her often.

And although Clay Tomlinson tonight wore a large white bandage over the left side of his head, and was apparently in some pain from his mishap, he was an amiable guest for supper.

Sarah cast her eyes at Giles, napkin tucked under his chins, and the couple's daughter Betty, prim in her becoming frock. Then she took her seat at the foot of the table. "Thanks for the compliments on the food. I do try. The cook I hired took careful selecting, I assure you. It practically exhausted me."

"You did wonderfully, my dear," Giles Murdock said. "And here comes dessert!"

Myrt Kobald strained under the weight of the laden platter as she entered and set it down. Her body was still stiff from mistreatment at Frank Gideon's hands, but she felt lucky that her face had nearly healed. Now she laid out pudding portions in front of each diner silently.

When she came to Mistress Sarah, she fought to control herself. Myrt had been hearing for years of the banker's wife's stinginess toward household help. Now she knew the rumors were all too true.

"About the Paris fashions shown in the new *Century Magazine,* Priscilla?"

"Yes, Sarah," Mrs. Clay Tomlinson purred.

Mr. Tomlinson rolled his eyes to the ceiling, then at Giles Murdock, the man who'd summoned him earlier in the day, been insistent he come, despite the need to recuperate from a sliced ear. The banker was finishing off his pudding with relish, shoving back his chair.

"Clay, shall we adjourn to the parlor for brandy and cigars?"

"A fine idea, Giles."

The gentlemen left the ladies with their chitchat of bustles and chapeaus and stalked to sit beside the parlor hearth.

As soon as both men clutched bell-shaped snifters of Napoleon, Tomlinson hissed: "And what's Wendell want of us this time, damn him?"

"The usual," Murdock replied. Our unqualified support. I'm having to turn down an offer for the Spade 8 ranch: money out of my pocket as he grabs the mortgage and takes possession. But that's just the beginning, Tomlinson!"

The newspaperman's hand drifted to his bandaged ear, and he winced. "Go on. State the worst."

"Wendell's set to move violently against Jowett, the town's only hold-out to his rule. Now here's what the bank and newspaper are supposed to do about the Silver Horseshoe gambling hall—"

There was a soft rap-rapping from the darkness outside the window. Banker Murdock lifted his jowly head, eyes apprehensive. Then he crossed the room and drew the draperies aside.

"Let me in!"

"In through the window? What the hell—?" Then he recognized the shadowy form standing in his wife's petunia bed. Over his plump shoulder he hissed to Tomlinson. "Hollis Jowett's out there, and he's holding a shooting iron on me!"

"For God's sake open up, or he'll kill you!"

A minute later Jowett hauled his lean form over the sill. The gun in his fist was a long-barreled Colt Dragoon with a filed sight. The gambler used his free hand to hold a hanky to his mouth. He coughed into it.

"A little bird told me two of Wendell's toadies were gettin' together tonight." Jowett smiled in oily fashion. "Gents, I'm here to make it worth your while to change sides. In the morning my men'll move against that bastard in the hill mansion.

146

Tomorrow night Bitter Wash will be in *my* pocket, payin' its protection dues to *me*. I want you to help spring the trap."

Murdock glanced at Tomlinson. The newspaperman studied the carpet underfoot.

"We don't dare," the banker blurted. "And you'll never win this play of yours, Jowett! It's insane to try! Why, Bert Wendell is—"

Jowett's smile vanished like spring snow. "Just thought I'd give you the chance. Now you've dug your graves. Men! Get your asses in here!"

Two gunslingers swung over and into the room through the window. Each hardcase grabbed a trembling businessman. "Put 'em away quiet, like you said, boss?"

Jowett gave a nod.

"Hold on a minute—" Tomlinson began.

He never finished. Grimy hands closed on his and the banker's mouths, and the hardcases' knives drove under their jaws, twisting viciously. Tomlinson's and Murdock's faces blanched with the opening of their neck arteries, and life bled out in torrents, staining their shirts and frock coats crimson. The only sounds were soft thuds as the corpses were let slide to the floor.

In the silence Jowett coughed again. "As I promised, boys, we'll now enjoy the females. They're in the next room." He led the way to the connecting door and the others trailed him, bursting in on the middle-aged wives and the attractive daughter. "Ladies, if you don't fight us—well, things can go a mite easier than otherwise!"

Mild squawks of surprise broke out. "Who're

147

you men?"

"The thin one's that awful Mr. Jowett I've seen in town! Despicable saloonkeeper!"

"Mother, I'm frightened!"

The burlier, taller of the gunsels crossed the floor in two quick steps, took Priscilla Tomlinson by the coiffed hair and wrenched her to her knees. With his other hand he fumbled at his belt buckle. When his trousers dropped to expose his manhood, the woman gasped. "My God!"

She was interrupted by the ripping sound of cloth: Sarah Murdock's fine dress. The garment was rent down the bodice by the gunsel with the malformed potato nose. Enormous melon breasts popped forth, but the man continued tearing petticoats and corset till the woman was stripped. Undismayed by the whalebone-stay markings on blubbery flesh, he shoved her to the floor and knelt between her thighs. Anguished groans flowed from her mouth as he proceeded to pump violently.

By this time Hollis Jowett, thin of frame as he was, had stripped off his frock coat and dropped it, then backed Betty into a corner. She cringed next to a six-foot china cupboard. "Keep away from me!" the young woman shrieked.

A wheezing cough drooled pink phlegm down the gambler's chin. "Gal, you got no choice." She tried to dodge the blow of his fist, but couldn't, so was flung into the cabinet, which teetered, then toppled with a shattering of glass. Cups, dishes and Tiffany doors dissolved to the floor in shivering shards.

Jowett's clawing hands hurled the girl down, and he flung up her skirts to drop on her.

"Oh, Mr. Jowett?" a calm female's voice said from the doorway. "Sorry to interrupt, but—"

Jowett's long jaw gaped, and he peered over his shoulder at Myrt.

"Christ, woman! I'm busy!"

"I've got more news for you that I overheard. I mean, besides the banker and the publisher comin' to this house to plot. Y'see—"

"If you want your bribe for tippin' me off, take the dollar from my coat pocket! Then get out!"

"But—"

He jerked a derringer from the watch pocket of his pants, aimed it across the flattened Betty.

"Jesus, I'm goin'! I'm goin'!"

As the door swung closed behind Myrt, she heard pained wails from three snobbish women she detested. She smiled because these were Wendell's friends, and hadn't Wendell put *her* through hell?

But as of now, neither did she care for Jowett and his cause.

The tight-fisted son of a bitch! Now she'd hold her tongue about Wendell's planned morning attack on the Silver Horseshoe. She snatched up Mrs. Murdock's jewels, wrapped in a napkin, and tucked the bundle under her arm.

Finally she could afford to leave town in style.

Chapter 19

As Cutter trailed the rugged route back toward Bitter Wash the morning sun hammered his back through his shirt. His stubbled face sweated, and he gave a curse for every mile trotted by the bay. No relief from the heat came from the blazing sky. The traveler baked in the rangeland's oven.

He'd be out of Texas soon, the big man assured himself. He was counting on it. There was satisfaction in yesterday's killing of the Wendell four, which meant the boss thug now had fewer to defend him. That had been the motive for the ambush, to deplete the guard. Next time Cutter would aim higher. Sometime Bert Wendell himself would be cut off from protection.

He fingered the garrote wire in his pocket. Maybe today would be that day.

In the saddle Cutter held his body rigid, his face carved in stoic, harsh lines. He was cautious as he rode, as always, eyes sweeping near and to the horizon, ears attuned to sounds, close or far. Such were rules of survival as taught by old Comanchero Ruiz.

For years he'd stayed alive through unrelenting watchfulness. Distrust had prevented linking up

150

with Jowett's type, ever. Now he grinned as he thought about it, and the grin was cruel as the brutal day's heat.

He topped a rise, saw the sprawl of town ahead and heard the faint sounds of gunfire.

Cutter gigged the horse into faster motion, galloping the last yards to the creek that flowed at the outskirts. He leaped from the saddle, snubbed reins to a bush, then yanked his Winchester from its boot. His pockets bulging with spare rounds, he dashed up the cutbank.

At first there were no people to be seen, but soon a man ran his way, followed by a sunbonneted woman. The female had a small child in tow. "If'n ya don't want trouble, mister, light a shuck! Th' big boys is fightin' in town! Boss Wendell's gunsels, Hollis Jowett's gunsels! Lordy!"

"In town? Whereabouts?"

But the scared people had moved quickly and vanished into the woods. Cutter spotted more fleeing folks among the houses at the town's edge, but not many, as if most were holed up to wait out bad times.

"Damned fools."

He lengthened his stride into a lope along the side street that paralleled the main drag. He passed a bootmaker's and a blacksmith's shop, and next a whitewashed school. No classes were in session. Cutter legged it into the alley alongside Madam Kate's brothel, and under the eyes of curious whores emerged onto boardwalk.

Shots were still peppering the street from behind porch stanchions, watering troughs and wagons.

151

Rifle and shotgun barrels poked through windows and pumped lead sporadically. Seeing wasn't easy through swirling powdersmoke. Now and again divots were chewed from the dirt and hurled. A half-dozen dead horses lay stretched beside hitch-rails.

The townsman at the creek had been correct: hell had broken loose in Bitter Wash. The trouble was, from behind gunsels' backs a stranger couldn't recognize enemies. As Cutter watched, a man clutching a rifle took a round and shrieked in pain. His form flopped from hiding behind a fire barrel. Another gunsel, twenty feet off, sprayed a pistol volley. Then a sniper on a roof cut him down.

A bullet whizzed by Cutter's ear, and he was stung by flung splinters from the clapboard wall. But an idea accompanied the cut cheek. The big man stepped through the door of the bawdy house. He found himself in a room garish with wall hangings, oak tables and plush settees.

Women lounged about the parlor house's parlor, half dressed. There were tall whores and stumpy whores, whip-thin and barrel-fat ones. Some wore black netlike wraps, some red, some yellow. The gal that cruised foremost across the floor was large-bosomed and purple-clad. Her rouged face grimaced.

"Sure, we got excitement for the fellas as come in here, mister. Long as you got greenbacks."

"I'm heading upstairs."

"Choose your partner."

"I pick Olivia, here." He hefted the carbine he

gripped.

"Wait — !"

The big man charged past the woman, and up the steps toward the second floor.

The second story was topped by an attic, and he climbed the narrow ladder leading to it without delay. Shouldering aside a trapdoor, he exited to the slanting roof. He could see fairly well from the elevation near the weathervane peak. It was a long way down.

Below, shootists were clustered in groups firing at will. The center of the battlefield seemed to be the Sunflower House Hotel. Three gunsels darted toward the large structure, were greeted by a hail of lead. One fellow, hit in the shoulder, back-pedaled with a shout, arm dangling uselessly. His pard's head took a load of double-aught buck, bloodsplash painting his shirt crimson. The last member of the threesome turned and scampered.

Cutter noted the vehicle that the coward dashed past: a nifty buggy with green-striped wheels. Bert Wendell's rig.

Cutter's violence-hardened mien broke into a smile. His enemy was there in the midst of town, leading his forces in person.

Now Cutter's task was to find the land-grabber and get him in his gunsights.

He swung into action. The next roof in the line belonged to Gardner's Merchandise Store. Adjoining that was Jowett's Silver Horseshoe, then the hotel. He jumped the gap to the next roof, a far from flat one, and landed with shingle-skidding bootsoles and a jangle of spurs, saving himself at the last second.

Hearing the scrape of steps, a crouching gunsel spun, showing a face that looked burro-stomped.

"Hey! What the—" The bore of the carbine swung toward Cutter. Cutter triggered from the hip, hit the jasper's arm, and blood flooded the hand around splinters of bone. Cutter shot again. This time the bullet split the man's nose, punched the head back with a snap, and sent him reeling back. He bounded off the store's eaves and plummeted to the street, splashing blood and torn sinew across the horses tethered below.

Cutter jumped the space between Gardner's and the Horseshoe.

Flinging back the trapdoor he landed beside, the big man lowered himself by a hand, then dropped. He'd managed to keep the Winchester in his grip, landing catfooted in the hall with the whores' cribs. He paused, and no noise broke the interior quiet. The shooting outside sounded like faint corn-popping in a pan.

Cutter moved to the end of the hall, then downstairs to what seemed the deserted main floor. The gambling wheels stood idle, and the bar was empty. A single lamp over the wide mirror threw dim light.

He started for the batwings. From outside the front of this saloon it was a mere frog's hop over to the hotel. Cutter meant to make that hop to get at Wendell and the chance for violent revenge.

"Hold it, you son of a bitch! Else you're ventilated!"

Now footfalls clattered from all sides as a dozen

grim-faced gunsels advanced on the big man. Some appeared from behind the bar, others from a storeroom, even the narrow aisle to the privy. Cutter recognized a few as Wendell's crew.

The bossman himself sauntered forth, in usual gait and form, his expression a scowl. He puffed his pipe as he spoke jeeringly. "My segundo Gideon saw you hit the roof above, fella, and we made a welcome party. I've been after your ass for days, mister."

Cutter stood still, not dropping the Winchester, not opening his mouth. Unwinking gun bores stared at him, the owners' features lit with evil delight. But the most pleased of all was Bert Wendell. "Frank, he hasn't dropped his rifle!"

A shot boomed in the confines, a bullet slamming the rifle's breech and spinning the weapon from Cutter. The gripping hand went numb from wrist to fingertips, although not broken. The hatred seethed in his brain. They'd seen him coming and laid a trap. He hadn't been expecting one in Jowett's headquarters.

The big man's face stayed blank as he said, "Wendell. We meet again, at last."

The eyes in the hatchet face glared intimidatingly. "You know me, it appears. But I don't know you. Wait a minute! Something familiar about your face—Men, close in on this bag of shit and take his sidearm!" To Cutter again: "A false move, and they've orders to swarm you! They'll beat you till you scream, and beyond! And I'll have me a merry laugh!"

As a gunsel with a barrel chest stepped toward

him, thick arms set to grab, Cutter backed against a table and bumped a chair. Now another hardcase moved in, this one smaller, rat-faced, savage-looking. Both men were clearly practiced roughnecks, entertaining no value for another's life.

Still, Cutter thought he saw a chance for himself. He dipped to one knee, lashed out with a hand, clasped the smaller foe's shirt to pull him in. He drove a fist deep in the runt's solar plexus, spun him and circled his neck with an arm. Gouging thumbs plowed voice box. "Jump me, and the jasper dies!"

"So be it! Watch out, Li'l Johnny!" Two other vicious-featured men leaped in with clubbed guns swinging. A blow meant for Cutter miscarried, and the stock of a Spencer carbine jolted Johnny's crown, coming away sticky with blood and hair. Cutter flung the slack form from him, clawed for his Colt, but was grabbed from behind and felt the weapon knocked down.

With Cutter's arm pinned back by a bearded giant's grip, another clean-shaven adversary pumped a kick to his groin. The shock wave of pain doubled him over. A fist slammed the back of his neck, powering him to the floor. He was able to launch a boot toe to the chin of a hunched attacker, but the jasper was replaced.

Three two-hundred-pound hardcases now squirmed atop him, pummeling with fists and knees—but he fought on. Pain only fueled him more. His raking thumb jellied an opponent's eye, a punching fist dislodged brown teeth to rattle like dice. But the battle was a lost cause. Frank Gideon fetched a cast-iron bootjack from the doorway, raised the heavy object, then brought it down on Cutter's skull.

He saw stars blaze across a field of black, and a hundred cannon roared.

He slumped facedown in the sawdust of the saloon floor, and knew no more.

Chapter 20

"Well, I'm damned," Bert Wendell snarled, his face twisted like that of a hungry predator. "I know you, after all, mister, and you're correct. No love's been lost between us in thirteen years, nor can there ever be! Damned bastard swine!"

Taking the caustic abuse groggily as consciousness flooded back, Cutter peered up from the saloon floor at the sneering boss of Bitter Wash. A mix of malevolence and wicked gloating, the white-suited gent's features hovered over the battered big man. "Sit him up," Wendell barked, and a hardcase propped Cutter's upper body against the bar. Only when he tried to move was he aware his wrists were tied behind him with rope. His shirt had been torn open down the front, revealing his chest with its powerful masculature.

On the right side the purple, puckered scar of his brand stood out, the large "C" framed in a ring, burned with the iron of the spread that had been his pa's.

"Young Jeb Cutter, all grown up." Bert Wendell leered sadistically. "Not to live much longer, though. You should've steered clear of Bert Wendell, my man. But, since you didn't have that sense, you'll be forced to pay!"

With a shuffling of boots the crew of gunsels surrounded the big man, faces draped in scowls. Scrapes, contusions and livid cuts adorned the crew, thanks to Cutter's fighting prowess, and the men seemed eager to even the score. A husky jasper with a bruised face leaned close, and Cutter was dragged across the floor. He was dropped beside a heap of smashed-up tables and chairs.

Wendell was there too, waving off flies drawn by the pools of congealing blood. "I aim to double my pleasure, Cutter," he said. "This saloon is—was—owned by my enemy Hollis Jowett. Unfortunately, he was absent when at sunup this morning my men moved in. Thus, we took over the place easily, before the counterattack you saw in the street. Still, before long I'll have the polecat defeated, strung by thumbs for daring to challenge me. Meanwhile—"

A pause.

"Meanwhile, Cutter," the land-grabber gloated, "I'll continue wreaking my dire hell! You never learned from that brand I burned on your hide, nor from seeing your father die. You'll get your real lesson today. My plan's been to burn Jowett's saloon down with you in it."

He turned to a chinless gunsel with a freckled brow. "Garrity, you're good at burning ranch houses and the like, so you'll make good with this duty. Wait till I and the others get out safe, then use lamp oil and torch the furniture and Cutter's

159

clothes." Wendell's face twitched with his excitement. He snatched a lamp from the bar, hurled it amid wrecked furniture to shatter there. The strong smell of kerosene rose.

Wendell, Frank Gideon and most of the crew filed out the rear door, laughing.

That left Garrity.

His mole-like mug wreathed in a malicious grin, the Irishman tugged lucifers from his pocket and showed them to Cutter. "Aye, 'tis a sorry day for ye, bastard." He pointed to his swollen lip. "Delighted I be, payin' back the hurt ye gave. Reckon the boss and boys are in the clear by now—"

"Hold on!"

Garrity sneered. "Gonna beg? That gives me a laugh! Haw!" He touched thumbnail to phosphorous tip, ready to strike the match.

"How much does Wendell pay you, Garrity? I'll give you plenty if you turn me loose. How'll your boss find out, since he'll think I died in a fire? I'm carrying bounty money I collected down Pecos way."

"Expect me to believe it? Haw!"

"You'd burn up two hundred dollars?"

A sidelong doubtful look. "That much? On you now?"

"In my left boot-top."

"I'll take a look."

As Paddy Garrity pocketed his lucifers and bent over Cutter's bound and contorted form, Cutter galvanized into deadly action. Lurching and arching himself powerfully, he drove bound legs up-

160

ward at the unsuspecting jasper's face. "What the bloody hell—?" The wedge-shaped bootheels slammed into the Irishman's face. Then, twisting his ankles, Cutter raked Garrity's face with the puncture tracks of the sharp rowels of his nickel-plated spurs. Each rowel-prick bloomed drops of blood. And then a spur sliced the staring, wide-open eye that it met, spurting gobs of water and blood. Garrity screamed. His hands at his eye sockets dragged through bloody stickiness, and the man went weak, fell. As soon as he was on the floor, Cutter kicked him again, smashed his nose, jammed his lips jarringly to broken teeth until Garrity was still. Then Cutter rolled to put his hands near the unconscious gunsel's knife and ease it from its sheath.

Within minutes the big man had slashed his bonds and gained his feet. Recovering his money, rifle and Colt required mere seconds, as did the checking of his cartridge loads. He jammed his banknotes in the same pocket as the coiled wire garrote. Garrity still lay sprawled with arms and legs outstretched, face immersed in puddled gore. Cutter stooped and scooped up a handful of spilled sulfur matches.

"Wendell expects a fire, and I aim to catch him unawares outside. Ain't got time to lug you around, Garrity. Looks like the payback you planned flashed in the pan." He scratched a light and dropped the match in slopped coal oil. Bright orange flames leaped ceilingward and across the floor. Cutter, exiting through the back, found no

161

Bert Wendell, no gunsels waiting outside.

He hotfooted it in the direction of the Sunflower, where he could still hear the popping of shots. He rounded a building corner and ran into Hollis Jowett, backed by sidekicks who fisted drawn guns.

"Cutter, by God! Have you seen Wendell? He surprised my people and took over the Silver Horseshoe while I was—er, otherwise occupied." The gambler coughed. "Now I aim to storm my place and occupy it again!"

"You're too late. The saloon's on fire."

"Christ! A kind of bastard that'd do that to a man!"

Jowett's visage was screwed up in hate. "Listen, Cutter, come fight on my side in this thing today. Sure, Wendell may have started out with more gunhands at his bidding, but we've whittled at 'em."

As the men spoke, there was fresh eruption of flurried gunfire. Cutter shouldered past Jowett and into the space between the saloon wall and the hotel. He could see horsemen galloping in the street, and glimpsed a skinny, white-coated figure in the midst of the charge.

Cutter broke into a run. Behind him he heard Jowett yelling, coughing, and yelling again. "Kill the sons of bitches! Damn! Goddamn!"

His face a mask of glistening sweat, Cutter leaped to the boardwalk and became witness to mass brutality.

Bullets swept the street and building fronts,

162

raining death on men and women caught in the crossfire. The unlucky ones were punched from running legs, thrown down or slammed into walls by drilling slugs. A drummer in a suit lost a leg to a shotgun blast and fell into a lung-shot homesteader's wife. A gray-haired old lady's skull exploded in a gory burst. A peachfuzz-faced youth ducked a round, but a window dissolved in shards that blinded him.

And the mayhem went on.

One of Jowett's faro dealers pumped hot lead from a Sharps pepperbox, but was killed in the doorway where he stood. A two-foot splinter protruded from his chest as he flopped across a woman's dead body. She lay among strewn intestines from a blown-open gut. From one end of Bitter Wash to the other, blood-caked corpses lay, glazed eyes fixed emptily on the sky.

The blazing Silver Horseshoe Saloon spouted flame from upper windows and various doors. Sooty clouds of smoke billowed to the heavens. Horses still alive and tied to hitchrails crowhopped in panic and lashed out with kicks. Shouts of "Conflagration!" and "My God!" rang out. Tongues of flame shot up walls, sparks spewed to alight on hotel and store roofs. More fire broke out on tinder-dry shingles there, and spread with lightning speed.

And at the far end of the street the riders were grouping again and reining about. Cutter saw their goal: to wipe out Jowett's resistance centered in the hotel.

163

Cries of the wounded shrilled in the baking air. "Charge!" Bert Wendell roared in a stentorian voice, clapping spurs to the leggy roan he straddled. Hoofbeats became a subdued thunder. Fanned into a surging formation that spanned the street, Wendell's gunsel cavalry charged.

Down the thoroughfare roared Wendell's army, pistols spitting death at all in their path. And yet Hollis Jowett's men opened up from windows and roofs, turning the street into a no-man's land raked by whistling bullets.

A head shot ripped the skull of one spurring jasper, catapulting him to the ground under an oncoming stallion's hooves. Sharp horseshoes shattered bones and burst skin. Another rider was blasted from the saddle, red rivulets staining his shirt and pants. A third's mount was shot in the haunch, flipping the man aboard into the side of a wagon. The gunsel's spine snapped loudly as he struck.

Bert Wendell waved a sixgun aloft, and yelled "Kill 'em! Kill the bastards!"

Cutter knelt on the boardwalk, threw his Winchester to his shoulder and began to toss hot lead. His first shot chewed the chest of the rider racing ahead of Wendell, shredding the man's flesh and splintering his ribs. His second shot punched the gunsel just to Wendell's left. This one's chin was obliterated in a crimson smear as blood sheeted down his front and across his mount's withers. Cutter next shot Wendell's horse, and the roan reared, gouting gore from a fist-sized hole opened in its belly. Then the animal toppled backward, dropping in the dust but concealing the rider.

"Damn it, bastard! Get up and show yourself!"

Into hoof-churning chaos galloped bold Frank Gideon astride a steeldust willing to be ridden through hell. The segundo stretched low to snatch Bert Wendell's arm, swung the man up with amazing strength to the saddle's cantle. Now Gideon rode, his boss clinging to his waist for life, coattails flying.

The tremendous stride of the horse sent it hurtling down on Cutter. The big man jacked out a spent cartridge and slammed another home, the Winchester cocked and ready.

Nine yards closed to six yards in the blink of a marksman's eye. Wendell was staring past Gideon's shoulder at Cutter, eyes bulging in his chalky face. Cutter's finger tightened on the trigger.

Excited shouts rang out: "The saloon front! It's about to cave! Look out!"

Gideon's gray sped near the boardwalk, its legs a flashing blur, then at the last instant, veered aside. Wendell, hanging on for his life, was almost unseated as the horse and riding pair swept past.

With a resounding crash like the collision of rushing trains, the façade of the Silver Horseshoe collapsed. Blazing chunks showered around Cutter, and a falling fagot deflected his rifle so that his bullet chewed dirt. The big man threw himself into a roll to avoid flying boards and slivered glass.

"Here comes another! Watch out!"

Cutter looked up and saw the towering sidewall of the saloon sway without support. Sparks spewed, flames shot forth, and a downdraft of furnace-hot air seared the big man's lungs. The wall tottered and burst into fragments while he watched, turned to a hell of raining fiery debris.

"The big stranger, he's gonna get crushed, by God!"

Chapter 21

Under the pelting of fireballs from the blazing saloon, Cutter kicked into his hardest roll yet, down and off the sidewalk in front of the Silver Horseshoe. He landed in street dust, amid a conflux of flame and smoke. The noise of the fire and collapsing walls roared in his ears. Powering to his legs, the big man tripped on a split duckboard and almost fell. But he managed to keep pumping, despite hot air that seared his lungs.

Shouts for help continued to ring, as did painful curses. Injured people raised a clamor of screams. The endangered men and women ran in panic as the blaze devoured their town. Wrecked, charred structures, horse and human remains all lay heaped on every side.

Cutter burst from the curtain of smoke and viewed the climax of the gunsel war that had sparked the fracas. Hardcases in the employ of Hollis Jowett roamed the business district, mopping up. When they found wounded Wendell men, they pumped hot lead in them until they were dead. Cutter moved along the street between leaping walls of fire, dripping sweat from every pore. He loped past bullet-riddled corpses and men dying from ghastly burns. One particularly battered body he recognized as the town barber. Flames crackled eerily in the background. Glowing ash drifted in the sky.

Then cries of "Christ, they're back!" were lofted, and added to the outcries were the drummings of galloping horses' hooves. Cutter spun. The gray horse straddled by Gideon and Wendell was racing with express-train speed. Cutter responded coolly, jerking his sixgun and triggering it.

In the middle of the street against a backdrop of towering flames he stood and rattled off his shots. Then, the Colt Frontier was empty, and the hightailers were streaking off unscathed. Desperately he scooped a shotgun from a stiff dead man's grip. He threw the weapon to his shoulder and opened up at Wendell, but the unfamiliar gun threw to the left.

The devastating blast of buckshot tore into Frank Gideon's frame, erasing an arm plus a great double-handful of torso flesh. A chewed cave trailing bloody tendons and gouting arteries remained. The segundo's corpse sailed off the horse leaving a blood-slick saddle that Wendell hauled himself onto. Now Jowett's men, too, were shooting in ragged fusillade, but Wendell spurred the gray around the bank corner, and was gone.

"Shit!"

Cutter moved fast. He sprinted toward the best horse he could spot: a sturdy Morgan at the hitchrail outside the jail. He vaulted aboard over the mount's rump.

"Hey!" croaked Sheriff Quade from within. The

168

lawman staggered to the doorway, brandishing a bottle.

The big man clapped spurs to the animal's flanks, and it charged off spiritedly. Cutter bent low over the surging neck, face stung by the thick mane, riding for all he was worth.

Reloading his sixgun at a wild gallop was fumbling work, but somehow he managed it. Still, the Colt was no long-range weapon, and he'd need to overtake and bring his quarry close — and soon. The Morgan wasn't as deep-bottomed and stout-winded as it first appeared. The sheriff had neglected its exercise. Its pace was faltering.

And they hadn't yet passed the Bitter Wash outskirts.

Far ahead along the wagon road south Cutter spied Wendell atop his long-legged gray horse. He could do nothing but ride and try to shorten the distance.

He spurred on.

Under the high, hot sky of cobalt blue the stocky Morgan ran, mesquite and sage clumps along the roadside dissolved in blurs to the eyes of the big man. Cutter, besides using spurs, lashed the gelding with long rein ends to urge speed. Dust pluming from the hooves of Wendell's mount remained a pillar to pursue.

And Cutter gained on the vicious jasper he chased. But Wendell turned from the road, up a serpentining trail into gully-broken hills. Cutter followed, and discovered steep going. Mesquite

169

branches as sharp as talons tore at him and his lathered mount.

Then for whole minutes, sight of the pursued was lost. A loaf-shaped fold of ground rose up which the Morgan labored, then finally topped. When Cutter pushed the horse over, a bee-buzz whine sang near his ear and his hat cartwheeled off crazily.

Ambush!

He jumped from the saddle and hit the ground running, spurts of dirt dusting his flying feet. A bullet tugged his sleeve. The big man dove and rolled—and spotted Wendell's position.

The varmint stood neck-deep in a dry and brushy gulch, his arm outstretched, sixgun cocked for another shot. The sun gleamed on the bald, sweat-beaded head, and the gray mustachios twitched. Beyond the man lay the foundered steeldust where it had dropped, gasping and thrashing.

A tiny cookfire smoldered nearby, smoke threading upward in a smear. There was a tumbledown line shack with its only window paneless. No other person seemed to be about.

The report of the rifle cut the air and again hot lead sped close to Cutter. Menaced by deadly crossfire, he hit the dirt, worming on belly and elbows until he got behind an outcrop. He fisted Ruiz's trusty Colt and calculated.

Wendell had led him into a trap. This line camp was on land that belonged to Wendell. The rifleman-cowboy worked for him.

He peeped from cover and watched the window

of the shack. The gunsmoke floating there gave the rifleman away. Then suddenly there was movement, and a wiry kid came through the door with a Henry carbine leveled from his waist.

"I'm gonna c'lect the bounty you promised, Mr. Wendell," the kid called. "Kill the bastard you hate. That twenty dollars'll buy the first night I ever had with a gal—at Roxie's!"

A grunt of surprise rose from the gulch. "Gil Jones, don't be too eager! That fella we got pinned down, he's mean! A varmint dangerous as they come—"

Casually, ignoring the stupidity written on the round face, Cutter shot the youth. The bullet tore past his ribs, buried in his heart, and he dropped like a chopped tree to lie unmoving. The kid had been no gunsel heavyweight. Before the dead boy hit the dirt, the big man was up from his dig-in and charging Wendell, who rushed off a last shot. The slug troughed Cutter's cheek below his eye, and he felt blood wash his face. He launched himself headlong and dove into Wendell, a powerful shoulder making impact with the scrawny chest and almost caving it in.

"Cutter, I'll pay you to let me live! Anything! Name your price!"

"My price is your hide!" A massive fist met Wendell's beak, flattening it like a spoon-bashed pancake. Backhanding, Cutter cuffed an ear, nearly ripping it from his foe's head. He pumped a knee to Wendell's groin, and the gent's legs buckled.

Fear filled Wendell's eyes, and his face twitched

spasmodically, a horrific mask. Cutter's gaze shot ferocious hatred as his grip yanked the man erect. Knuckles slammed the writhing mouth, and demolished teeth crunched. Chips of enamel drove down Wendell's gullet, and gobs of blood spurted over ripped lips.

"Cutter, I'm pleading—"

Cutter had pulled from his pocket the short length of wire he used for a garrote. A shake of the wrist uncoiled the instrument of death. With fiendish efficiency he looped the neck of the terrorized man, drew the wire tight, then even tighter. The land-grabber's breath was cut off. The hollow cheeks reddened and turned plum-colored, and the eyes bugged hugely. Veins in Wendell's throat stood out like worms. The blackened tongue thrust out and wagged.

Then Bert Wendell went limp, and shuddered in a parody of dance. Cutter relaxed the wire, and the choked man slumped to the ground, lifeless.

Cutter straightened up, snarled, and stalked across the yard toward the cabin. He emerged in less than a minute holding a branding iron with a head in the shape of a "W."

This he inserted among the coals of the fire, stirring briskly, then hunkered down beside it. A slow quarter-hour dragged by, and Cutter fingered the brand that scarred the skin beneath his shirt.

A picture of his murdered pa's corpse rose in his brain. It was again thirteen years ago to him. Recollection of Bert Wendell joined the vision, and the land-grabber seemed to laugh maniacally.

Cutter pulled out the now hot iron, its head

radiating a bright glow. He walked to where Wendell lay, planted the cherry-red face of the iron on the dead chest, where it seared through clothes, then into skin that flaked and smoked. A hideous, cloying odor filled the air for yards. There were no sounds, not of birds or four-footed creatures. Only the hissing of hot iron touching human flesh.

ED MCBAIN'S MYSTERIES

JACK AND THE BEANSTALK   (17-083, $3.95)
Jack's dead, stabbed fourteen times. And thirty-six thousand's missing in cash. Matthew's questions are turning up some long-buried pasts, a second dead body, and some beautiful suspects. Like Sunny, Jack's sister, a surfer boy's fantasy, a delicious girl with some unsavory secrets.

BEAUTY AND THE BEAST   (17-134, $3.95)
She was spectacular—an unforgettable beauty with exquisite features. On Monday, the same woman appeared in Hope's law office to file a complaint. She had been badly beaten—a mass of purple bruises with one eye swollen completely shut. And she wanted her husband put away before something worse happened. Her body was discovered on Tuesday, bound with wire coat hangers and burned to a crisp. But her husband—big, and monstrously ugly—denies the charge.

Available wherever paperbacks are sold, or order direct from the Publisher. Send cover price plus 50¢ per copy for mailing and handling to Pinnacle Books, Dept.17-378, 475 Park Avenue South, New York, N.Y. 10016. Residents of New York, New Jersey and Pennsylvania must include sales tax. DO NOT SEND CASH.

ESPIONAGE FICTION BY WARREN MURPHY AND MOLLY COCHRAN

GRANDMASTER   (17-101, $4.50)
There are only two true powers in the world. One is goodness. One is evil. And one man knows them both. He knows the uses of pleasure, the secrets of pain. He understands the deadly forces that grip the world in treachery. He moves like a shadow, a promise of danger, from Moscow to Washington—from Havana to Tibet. In a game that may never be over, he is the grandmaster.

THE HAND OF LAZARUS   (17-100, $4.50)
A grim spectre of death looms over the tiny County Kerry village of Ardath. The savage plague of urban violence has begun to weave its insidious way into the peaceful fabric of Irish country life. The IRA's most mysterious, elusive, and bloodthirsty murderer has chosen Ardath as his hunting ground, the site that will rock the world and plunge the beleaguered island nation into irreversible chaos: the brutal assassination of the Pope.

Available wherever paperbacks are sold, or order direct from the Publisher. Send cover price plus 50¢ per copy for mailing and handling to Pinnacle Books, Dept.17-378, 475 Park Avenue South, New York, N.Y. 10016. Residents of New York, New Jersey and Pennsylvania must include sales tax. DO NOT SEND CASH.